THE OT

CW00555178

JOHN BOYNTON PRIESTLEY was
schoolmaster. After leaving Belle
in a wool office but was already ~, ~~~ ~~~~ determined to become a
writer. He volunteered for the army in 1914 during the First World War
and served five years; on his return home, he attended university and
wrote articles for the *Yorkshire Observer*. After graduating, he established
himself in London, writing essays, reviews, and other nonfiction, and
publishing several miscellaneous volumes. In 1927 his first two novels
appeared, *Adam in Moonshine* and *Benighted*, which was the basis for
James Whale's film *The Old Dark House* (1932). In 1929 Priestley scored
his first major critical success as a novelist, winning the James Tait
Black Memorial Prize for *The Good Companions*. *Angel Pavement* (1930)
followed and was also extremely well received. Throughout the next
several decades, Priestley published numerous novels, many of them
very popular and successful, including *Bright Day* (1946) and *Lost Empires*
(1965), and was also a prolific and highly regarded playwright.

Priestley died in 1984, and though his plays have continued to
be published and performed since his death, much of his fiction has
unfortunately fallen into obscurity. Valancourt Books is in the process of
reprinting many of J. B. Priestley's best works of fiction with the aim of
allowing a new generation of readers to discover this unjustly neglected
author's books.

JOHN BAXENDALE is Principal Lecturer in Social and Cultural History at
Sheffield Hallam University. He is the author of *Priestley's England: J. B.
Priestley and English Culture* (Manchester University Press, 2008).

FICTION BY J. B. PRIESTLEY

Adam in Moonshine (1927)
Benighted (1927)★
Farthing Hall (with Hugh Walpole) (1929)
The Good Companions (1929)
Angel Pavement (1930)
Faraway (1932)
Wonder Hero (1933)
I'll Tell You Everything (with Gerald Bullett) (1933)
They Walk in the City (1936)
The Doomsday Men (1938)★
Let the People Sing (1939)
Blackout in Gretley (1942)
Daylight on Saturday (1943)
Three Men in New Suits (1945)
Bright Day (1946)
Jenny Villiers (1947)
Festival at Farbridge (1951)
The Other Place (1953)★
The Magicians (1954)★
Low Notes on a High Level (1954)
Saturn Over the Water (1961)★
The Thirty First of June (1961)★
The Shapes of Sleep (1962)★
Sir Michael and Sir George (1964)
Lost Empires (1965)
Salt is Leaving (1966)★
It's an Old Country (1967)
The Image Men: Out of Town (vol. 1), *London End* (vol. 2) (1968)
The Carfitt Crisis (1975)
Found Lost Found (1976)

★ Available from Valancourt Books

J. B. PRIESTLEY

THE OTHER PLACE

AND OTHER STORIES OF THE SAME SORT

With an introduction by
JOHN BAXENDALE

VALANCOURT BOOKS

The Other Place by J. B. Priestley
First published London: Heinemann, 1953
First Valancourt Books edition 2013
Reprinted 2018

Copyright © 1953, renewed 1981 by J. B. Priestley
Introduction © 2013 by John Baxendale

Published by Valancourt Books, Richmond, Virginia
http://www.valancourtbooks.com

ISBN 978-1-948405-11-9 (trade paperback)
ISBN 978-1-948405-12-6 (hardcover)

Also available as an electronic book and an audiobook.

All Valancourt Books publications are printed on acid free paper that meets all ANSI standards for archival quality paper.

Cover by Henry Petrides
Set in Dante MT

INTRODUCTION

J. B. PRIESTLEY (1894-1984) was one of the most celebrated and prolific English writers of his time. Over thirty novels, as many plays, and a continuous stream of essays, journalism, film-scripts and radio broadcasts kept him in the public eye from the 1920s to the 1970s. Priestley's novels such as *The Good Companions* (1929), *Angel Pavement* (1930), or *Bright Day* (1946) explore large themes across a broad canvas teeming with characters. His more concentrated and focused ideas usually became plays. Short stories were perhaps his least favourite literary form, but he never lacked ideas, and over the years some of them ended up in this form. Reissuing this book in the 1960s Priestley's British publishers gave it a new subtitle, "Stories on the Edge of the Marvellous", and that is what they are, thoughtful entertainments with more than a touch of the supernatural. Priestley once said of the painter Pieter Brueghel that lurking behind the sharply-observed detail of his pictures of peasant life is a "fairy-tale country . . . poised on the edge of marvels and miracles . . . feeling a trifle haunted", and the same could be said of these stories: their tales of the uncanny and the downright impossible are (with one exception) set against the sharply-observed detail of ordinary post-war English life, and this is one of their pleasures. But although they work perfectly well as entertainment and social observation they go a bit deeper than that too, drawing upon some challenging ideas about time and human psychology to express Priestley's anxieties about the direction Britain was taking after the traumas of war and reconstruction. Reading them we encounter not only an accomplished entertainer, but also a politically engaged social observer, as well as a semi-mystical visionary.

These stories stand alone as thought-provoking entertainments, but some historical context helps us to understand where they are coming from. Priestley had always been a political as well as a literary animal. Raised in the radical and socialist climate of the Yorkshire industrial town of Bradford, he turned to social and political themes in his novels of the 1930s and in *English Journey* (1934), his masterly account of England in the Slump, which predates and in many ways outdoes the more celebrated work of George Orwell. The first readers of these stories would remember his recent wartime BBC radio broadcasts, as popular as Churchill's, in which he prefigured a better, more co-operative world after the war: if we could all work together to defeat Hitler, surely we could do the same to build a better Britain. By 1952, when all but one of these stories was written, that vision was fading, and several of these stories express this feeling of anxiety and disillusion. Priestley had enthusiastically supported the Labour Party in its landslide election victory in 1945, and took part in its campaign for re-election in 1950, welcoming the changes the government had brought about. But his socialism, humanistic and libertarian, was about building a new world from the bottom up—"Out of the People", as one of his wartime pamphlets put it, quoting Walt Whitman. The Labour government's approach, shaped by wartime experience, was more in the top-down Fabian tradition, emphasising the role of a strong but benevolent state working through large national organisations like the National Health Service. Priestley feared that, while doing good, this approach disempowered people just as much as corporate capitalism. Perhaps instead of the old power-structures being swept away, new ones had been created which sat all too easily alongside them.

In 1952, Britain was on the cusp of another revolution which Priestley also found disturbing: the onset of mass consumerism in the long boom of the 1950s and '60s—indeed, the emerging medium of television plays a key role in one of these stories. Priestley welcomed the fact that people were better off, but had serious misgivings about the kind of society that affluence brought with it. In 1954 during a visit to the United States, he would coin the term Admass to describe the combination of materialism, advertising, mass communication and mass culture which he feared was creating "the mass mind, the mass man", and preventing people from realising their true potential. This anxiety too finds its way into these stories.

The summer of 1952, when all but one of these stories were written, was a difficult time in Priestley's own life. He was going through a divorce, and although this was the prelude to a long and happy third marriage to the archaeologist Jacquetta Hawkes, the transition was traumatic and frustrating. He described in his memoir *Margin Released* (1962) how the act of writing had helped him through an earlier moment of far greater anguish: by working on something completely unconnected with his own situation, "I wrote myself out of my misery, followed a trail of thought and words into daylight"; perhaps these stories came out of a similar experience. There is more than an echo here of the Russian philosopher Ouspensky's psychological doctrine of "non-identification"; Priestley had encountered Ouspensky's writing on a visit to California in the 1930s, and we know he was re-reading him around the time these stories were written. Ouspensky also had unorthodox ideas about time, a topic which had fascinated Priestley since he first read J. W. Dunne's *An Experiment with Time* in the 1920s. Through these writers, Priestley came to question the orthodox idea of time as a single irreversible flow, suggesting instead a series of parallel streams, with the possibility of the observer shifting from one to the other—particularly, as Dunne suggested, in dreams. Priestley was to explore his own ideas about time in *Man and Time* (1964), but they had already made themselves felt in his plays, most notably *Dangerous Corner* (1932), *Time and the Conways* (1937) and *I Have Been Here Before* (1937), and they can be found throughout the stories in this collection, no doubt inspired by his re-encounter with Ouspensky.

As with his "time plays", we might well ask how far these time-shifts and alternative realities are really a deep exploration of the nature of time, or whether they are simply used as narrative devices to allow Priestley to make his points about people and society. These two sides of Priestley, the mystic visionary and the social critic, while not exactly in conflict, can often pull in different directions. At bottom, Priestley the novelist was a realist, writing as the nineteenth-century masters did about people in society, and at odds with the more fashionable modernism with its poetic introspection and its preoccupation with language and form. For this reason it was the social critic who usually won out, although the fact that his social critique was rooted in the individual and the human character rather than in the class struggle or the great movements of history meant that there was always a subjective, introspective aspect to his fiction which allowed his mystical side to have its say; the novel *Bright Day* (1946) is a good example of this, and in perhaps his best-known play, *An Inspector Calls* (1945), his sense of the uncanny and the unexplained is effectively deployed in support of a powerful political message.

We can see this combination at work in the title story, "The Other Place". The idea of an idyllic world, once ours but now lost to us because of our human failings, is of course a recurring theme in our culture from the Book of Genesis to Shangri-La. This "other place" is more personalised, built around the yearnings and better nature of the story-teller, Lindfield, and lost through his failure to live up to them. Priestley did not believe in utopias, but he did believe that humanity, if not perfectible, could at least be improved, and that the source of this improvement lay within us. In the Battle of Britain summer of 1940, that moment of "noble common purpose", he thought he had caught a glimpse of how that could be, and it is possible that the story reflects his disillusion at the loss of that dream. Perhaps also he is suggesting that instead of searching hopelessly for "The Other Place" as Lindfield does we should settle for the real-world idyll of Hubberholme, the Yorkshire village Priestley loved, where the story begins and where his ashes were to be buried, under a quotation from the first sentence of this book.

In "The Grey Ones" Priestley gives early expression to his fears for the post-war world. Mr. Patson is thought insane because he has a vision—that the world is being taken over by alien beings, the eponymous Grey Ones, whose purpose is to wipe out all "wonder, joy, deep feeling" and turn mankind into "mass beings without individuality, soulless machines". This is undoubtedly a vision of "Admass", and also of what Priestley would later label "Topside", the new post-war ruling class which stood for nothing but itself and imposed stability and sterility on a nation in need of creativity and passion. Patson may indeed be insane, but beneath his lurid vision of giant alien toads there lies a more mundane but equally threatening reality, which only the visionary can see for what it is.

"Uncle Phil on TV", for me the most entertaining of these stories, is about a haunted TV set. BBC television broadcasts, begun in 1936, had resumed after the war, but only at the end of the 1940s were they becoming accessible outside London; within a decade TV would be a universal part of everyday life, the cornerstone of Priestley's "Admass". Priestley's deft touch with the mundane details of life delivers some rare glimpses of that moment of transition: the high cost of the set (£120 in 1952 is over £2500 (around $4000) in today's money); uncertainty about how you watch it (in solemn silence like in a theatre, or as a continuous background to domestic life); how and when you invite the neighbours in to watch (a common quandary for early adopters); the unfamiliarity of TV programmes before they had bedded in to everyday life. But although Uncle Phil snarls from beyond the grave that the country's full of zombies these days, we are not yet being invited to blame TV for that state of affairs.

In "Guest of Honour", we are back to the world of "Topside", with an added twist invoking the forking paths of time, and a hint of Priestley's belief that people could and should be better than they are. There's a robust satirical portrait of a pompous industrialist whose deranged visions, a punishment for his self-importance, match those of Patson in "The Grey Ones". Like the family in Priestley's first play, *Dangerous Corner*, who are whisked back in Act Three to the source of what went wrong with their lives, Sir Bernard is given a second chance; but the ending is problematic. Is his return to "normal" really some kind of redemption? Wouldn't it be better if he continued to see things as they really are?

"Look After the Strange Girl" is a time-displacement story set in familiar Priestley territory. The Edwardian world in which Mark finds himself is the world of Priestley's youth, a world of promise shattered by war which he often revisited in his writing. The story gives an entertaining account of upper-class life in 1902, making play with differing social mores of 1902 and 1952, and bringing out the asymmetrical nature of time travel: the Edwardians are recognisable as such to Mark, while to them he merely seems odd. But as always with Priestley what might be nothing more than an exercise in nostalgia enlivened by a spot of time-travel carries an undertone of desolation and loss. As in *Bright Day* and *An Inspector Calls*, among others, we see a society headed for destruction without knowing it. Through Priestley's manipulation of the time-frame Mark knows what is going to happen to these people and their world, but there is nothing he can do about it. Fortunately he can console himself with a happy ending.

Like Mark, and like Patson in "The Grey Ones", Walter Voley in "The Statues" has knowledge which those around him lack: perhaps knowledge of the future, perhaps only the realisation that life could be finer and nobler than it is—a realisation, in several of these stories, granted only to a few, who are regarded by others as strange or even mad, and to whom it brings only futility and despair. Voley's colleague Saunders suggests that he might be seeing the future, and recommends some reading—presumably Dunne and Ouspensky—which might help him get on top of his experience, but he is having nothing to do with "fantastic theories". It is in the end the contrast between Voley's grubby trivial world of popular journalism and the nobility of his visions which does for him, and at the same time evokes Priestley's own lost visions of a better world.

With "The Leadington Incident" we are on similar territory to "Guest of Honour". Sir George Cobthorne meets an unassuming stranger on a train who is annoyingly unimpressed by his own eminence, and succeeds in undermining his belief in his "Topside" world, bringing on nightmare visions comparable to Patson's in "The Grey Ones", though not so lurid. Sir George comes to see that "the only people who were alive and awake . . . were a few odds and ends of nonentities", and the intervention of such "nonentities", superficially unimpressive strangers, is a recurring device in these stories: the semi-oriental baronet who shows Lindfield the way to The Other Place; the shabby old man nearly run over by Sir Bernard's Rolls-Royce; Cobthorne's "crumpled" stranger on the train. They are the ones who can show you how the world really is, but nobody pays any attention to them. The thing is not to be driven down by this knowledge like Voley, or like Mr. Strenberry in the next story.

"Mr. Strenberry's Tale" is the only story in this collection not written in 1952. It dates back to the summer of 1929, written presumably as a diversion while Priestley was hard at work on his first big best-seller, *The Good Companions*. Strenberry's vision of the future is not utopian, like Voley's, but prefigures nothing less than the destruction of mankind, a message delivered from the distant future by "a man—a sort of man" who is trying to escape his fate. No more than Voley can Strenberry deal with this knowledge of the future; no more than Mark in "Strange Girl" can he do anything with it; he ends up a dishevelled drinker in a pub. There are distinct echoes of H. G. Wells in this story—in particular the highly-evolved visitor from the future, reminiscent of "The Time Machine"—and Strenberry duly references Wells in his account.

The last and longest story in the collection is "Night Sequence". Two stranded travellers on a dark and stormy night seek refuge in an old house whose occupants are not quite as they seem: how many tales of the uncanny or the supernatural have begun that way, including Priestley's own early novel, *Benighted*? Yet this is not really a story about ghosts, or even about time-travel, but about Luke and Betty's troubled relationship and dissatisfied lives, and how that night's experience starts their healing process. We hear Priestley's voice more clearly in this story than any other: his interest in Jungian psychology expressed in a speech about the proper balance between male and female principles; his critique of the rat-race in Luke and Betty's determination to change their lives, to stop "jeering at and cheapening life" but to bring to it "energy and good humour and some sense of style". Nothing could be more typical of Priestley than this hope for change coming from within, inspired by a vision of a better life.

Nine stories, all very much of their time, all marked by Priestley's strong individual voice, his philosophical and political preoccupations, his skill at story-telling, and the well-observed detail which brings the story to life. As always with Priestley, there is plenty here to provoke deep thought, but there is also plenty to entertain—and often both at once.

JOHN BAXENDALE
Sheffield Hallam University
April 20, 2013

THE OTHER PLACE

Author's Note: The only story here that has been published in a book before is "Mr. Strenberry's Tale", which has appeared in various short-story anthologies and in a Pan miscellany of mine called *Going Up*. I have reprinted it here, although it was written years before the others, because it seems to me to belong to this collection of tales.—J.B.P.

Contents

THE OTHER PLACE

A SHORT walk beyond Buckden, in Upper Wharfedale, is Hubberholme, one of the smallest and pleasantest places in the world. It consists of an old church, a pub, and a bridge, set in a dale among high moors. In summer, long after the snows have melted, there is rarely much water in the river, so that it glitters and winks; and a man who has been walking for an hour or two can loiter on that bridge for quite a time, waiting for the pub to open and staring at the river. He was already there when I arrived—a big-boned dark fellow about forty—and he was looking down at the water in a glum fashion, without troubling to re-light the cigar he was chewing. Something had disappointed him, and I found it hard to believe Hubberholme had not come up to his expectations; so I spoke to him.

We agreed that it was a fine day, that this was good country; after which I thought I might try to satisfy my curiosity. So I told him how fond I was of Hubberholme, and how I rarely let a couple of years pass without taking another look at it. He said I was quite right, that he could easily imagine himself feeling the same way about it.

"But if you don't mind my saying so," I said, "you looked as if you'd found this place disappointing."

"Well, I guess I did," he said slowly. He had a deep voice and an accent that might have been American or Canadian. "But not in the way you mean, sir. Nothing wrong with this at all. Couldn't be better. But from the way a fellow described it to me, I thought it might be a place I've been trying to find. And it isn't, that's all." And now, perhaps because he did not want to say any more, he did re-light his cigar. But to show me that he was not unfriendly, he asked me where I was staying.

We discovered then that we were both spending the night

in the admirable village of Kettlewell, further down the Dale, but had booked ourselves at different inns. After some further chat we agreed not only to walk back to Kettlewell together but to dine too; and after pointing out that I was the older man and this was my country and not his, I made him agree to be my guest. On our walk back I learnt that his name was Harvey Lindfield, that he was an engineer from Toronto, that he had been married but was now divorced and had a small daughter at present living with his sister. He talked readily enough, and was clearly glad of company, but somewhere behind his talk there was a cloud, a shadow, which might be disappointment or bewilderment. It was not, however, until after dinner, when we lit our cigars in the little sitting-room we had to ourselves and drank the excellent rye whisky that he had brought over as his contribution to the evening's hospitality, that I ventured to suggest that something was troubling him. And I admitted that I was curious.

"You'll remember," I told him, "you said that Hubberholme might be a place you were trying to find." I left it at that, but looked him at expectantly.

"It's the damnedest thing," he confessed, staring at the frilled paper in the fire grate. "I can hardly believe it myself, so why should you? I tried telling it once and got stuck about halfway through. If you weren't a writer, I wouldn't risk it now. But you get around, you talk to people, you must know a lot of things happen that can't be explained. Okay—this is one of 'em. The damnedest thing ever. And don't think I could make it up," he continued, regarding me earnestly. "I wouldn't know where to start. Now if you were telling it to me, that 'ud be different. I wouldn't believe you. But I'm no writer, just a plain engineer, and you've got to believe me. I'll just freshen these drinks, then I'll tell it to you the best way I can." And this was the story he told me.

. . . . .

My company (Lindfield began) had ordered a machine from a firm in Blackley, and I was sent over to make sure this machine was what we wanted. Well, it wasn't. Do you want to know about this machine? No, I thought not. The point is—there wasn't a hell of a lot wrong with it, but just enough to keep me there in Blackley making sure they put it right. So there I was, stuck with the Blackley Electrical Engineering Company, and with Blackley. I forgot to say, this was last November.

Do you know Blackley? Yes—well, going through it is about as much as anybody'd want of Blackley. Especially last November, when it rained and rained and rained and if the sun ever rose and shone, I missed it. When they built that place, they must have wanted to punish themselves. It didn't matter how dark and wet a November might be, Blackley was ready to meet it halfway. It was still dark when I got up in the morning, and by four o'clock it was dark again, and in between it rained. Even when you went inside somewhere, pulled down the blinds and turned on the lights, you didn't feel you'd got any illumination. I thought at first my eyesight was going.

I stayed at the Railway Hotel, next to the station and with a nice view of the tracks and sidings. It was darkish and wettish in there too. I changed my room three times, thinking I'd get something better, but I never did. We ate in the Coffee Room, which had sideboards and dish covers and cruets and knives and forks big enough for a roasted ox, only we never had the roasted ox, just a few sad bits of meat and a lot of drowned vegetables. There was an old waiter, blue in the face from heart disease, and two sour-faced waitresses, one long and thin and the other short and thick, and both of 'em dead against us. The only time they looked pleased was when they could tell you something was 'off' or you were too late to have anything. The other fellows there were travelling salesmen, all oldish and defeated, not smart enough to use a car so that they wouldn't have to spend the night in the Railway Hotel, Blackley. After supper they used to sit in a gloomy little hole called the Residents' Lounge, writing long reports explaining why they hadn't taken any orders. It wasn't much better downstairs in the bar. All the customers down there were either earnestly whispering or just sitting staring at nothing. They made you feel somebody important had just died.

I'm not saying the whole town was really like that, but it did seem like that to me. Dark, wet, and dismal. Nothing to do, nowhere to go. It's not that I expected two miles of neon lighting every night and a Big City atmosphere. I've lived in small towns before, and anyhow Blackley wasn't that small— about seventy-five thousand people, I guess. But it hadn't anything for me that I wanted, except that machine I stared at every day, up at the Blackley Electrical Engineering works. On the inside, for somebody who'd properly settled there, the place might have been all right, but on the outside, where I was, it was a living death. If any people there were having a good time, they were doing it behind locked doors. Oh—there were amusements of a sort—a crummy little vaudeville theatre, three or four movie houses, a café where a lot of kids sat about with steaming clothes, and one gaudy big pub where a lot of middle-aged dough-faced whores waited for custom and listened to a blind pianist. I went home with one of 'em one night, but even with the load of gin and whisky I was carrying I couldn't make it, and had to tell her I was meeting a late train. What I did meet—and it took some facing—was that bedroom, cold as organised charity, in the Railway Hotel. I'd have met anybody, getting off any train, just for a change. It was bad enough during the week but Sunday was worse. If I'm ever sent to Hell, it won't be all flames and sulphur and roaring devils; it'll be the Railway Hotel, Blackley, on a wet November Sunday that lasts for ever.

I know what you're thinking—that I didn't give the place a chance, never tried to make the best of it. But I did. Yet somehow I'd no luck. The fellows up at the works were friendly enough—after all, I represented a big order they wanted badly—but even when we all tried, we never got going. The two I saw most of, on the job, Butterworth and Dawson, nice fellows about my own age, took me home and gave me dinner or supper, introduced me to some neighbours, made me talk about Canada, turned on their TV or arranged some bridge. They did their best and so did their wives, but it didn't really work out, perhaps because by that time I felt so dam' lonely and lost I wanted more than I'd a right to expect. I still felt way off on the outside, and couldn't break through. If I tried, got a bit personal, I felt they drew back. It was like calling somewhere when all the people in the house are worried about something, an illness they don't want you to know about or a daughter who's got herself engaged to the wrong man, and they're polite and doing their best but can't really attend to you with most of their minds. So I'd leave 'em feeling more out of it than when I went. Yet I had the notion even then—and you'll understand soon why I say *even then*—that fellows like Butterworth and Dawson might have been real friends if we could only have got rid of the glass wall between us.

I'm no chaser—and as I told you this afternoon I'd had one marriage I was glad to get out of—but it's only natural, especially when a man feels so lonely and out of it, to see if there isn't a woman who might help. And that doesn't just mean a package of sex, as too many people seem to think. There's more in being with a woman than that, though it has to find its place of course. Well, I got to know a woman—she was personnel manager at another works and happened to step across to the Blackley Electrical Engineering place when I was there. Her name was Mavis Gilbert and she was in her early thirties, tallish, dark, good profile, with something pleasant and sensible about her. I took her to the movies once or twice or we met for a drink, and one night she gave me supper where she lived. But that didn't work out either. In fact it made things worse, not better. There was some fellow she couldn't forget, and when she'd had a couple of drinks or had been softened up by a sentimental movie, she didn't even try to forget him.

Round about ten-thirty a little lost puppy would come and look out of her eyes. I dare say she'd have let me make love to her, if I'd made an issue out of it; but I knew there wouldn't have been anything gay about it, just awkwardness and apologies and then some quiet sobbing after I'd gone; so I didn't press her, which must have been a relief to her but didn't do me much good. In fact, just because she was a nice girl who ought to have been fairly happy and wasn't, who could feel herself getting drearier and couldn't stop it, she made me feel worse; and by the third week I wasn't seeing her any more but killing the nights with a mixture of hard liquor and fairly soft reading matter. And it still rained, and, as far as I could tell, the sun went out altogether. Sometimes I wondered if I was dead.

Then, just when I'd decided nothing could ever happen again, something happened. One afternoon about five, on my way back from the works, I was crossing the square in front of the railway station, to reach the hotel, when I saw a little old fellow slip and fall with a truck almost on top of him. If he'd been fifty pounds heavier I couldn't have done it, but he couldn't have weighed more than a hundred and twenty; and I jerked him out of the way just in time. I took him into the hotel, made them give him some brandy, and helped to clean the mud off him. He told me he was Sir Alaric Foden; and he was a baronet, though he didn't look like my idea of a baronet. He'd spent most of his life, before he came into the title and the family property, out in India and the Far East; and I'd say that either his mother or one of his grandmothers had been a native of those parts, because his eyes were like black beads floating in yellow oil and looked about as English as the Taj Mahal. His wispy hair and little beard were white, and his face might have been a withered leaf. He always spoke very slowly and with an effort, as if his talking mechanism had got rusted up, and while he kept you waiting for the next word he fixed his black little eyes on you, with hardly a blink, until you began to feel you were already in India or China or somewhere. He was obviously grateful and made a fuss about what I'd done, yet at the same time he didn't give me the impression of being really friendly, though perhaps by then Blackley had made me morbid on the subject. When he found out I wasn't doing anything the next night—and that didn't take long—he asked me to go out to his house and dine with him. He lived about ten miles out, but there was a bus service within a few minutes' walk. I would have to leave about nine-forty-five to get the bus back, but he thought that would give me long enough with him. And so did I.

From now on it's a peculiar story, and I'll have to slow up a bit and take it steady. As I said earlier, I've never told it yet all the way through. I can't decide yet whether I ought to rattle off everything I can remember or sort it out and just give you the high spots. Yes, being a writer you must understand the kind of difficulty, so you won't mind if I stop now and again to see where I'm going and whether I'm putting too much in or leaving too much out. And help yourself to a drink, won't you? Yes, I might as well. Thanks.

Well, sir, the next night I went out by bus and found my way to the country mansion of Sir Alaric Foden, Bart. If I was making this up I'd tell you now what a wonderful place it was and what a fine reception I had, with footmen waiting on us and caviare and champagne cooling nicely in buckets. But it wasn't like that. Oh—it was a mansion all right, though I never saw most of it, and I doubt if Sir Alaric had for some time. But what I did see was damp, chilly and shabby, and you couldn't have paid me to live there. No footmen, not even a butler, only a wheezy old woman to wait on us. And the dinner might have been sent out from the Railway Hotel, all except the wine, which Sir Alaric said was one of his best clarets. He took only about half a glass and made me finish the rest, which I did, not in the dining-room, all cold and cheerless, but upstairs in the library, where there was a fire. It was a big room, and must have had thousands of books in it as well as enough Oriental stuff to stock a curio shop. All through dinner and just afterwards up there he told me very little about himself, but made me talk, chiefly by asking me what I thought about Blackley and how I was doing there. I'm not going to tell you what I said because you've heard most of it already.

"So, Mr. Lindfield," he said when I had talked myself out, "you are—unhappy—in Blackley. Or—at least—bored—depressed—lonely. You would like—to visit—some other place—humph?"

I said I would, but pointed out that just then I hadn't the time or opportunity, having to keep an eye on that machine.

"The time—that is nothing," he said; and he waved a claw at a lacquered grandfather clock as if to abolish it and time. "The opportunity—might be here. Yes—in this room. That is—if you are ready—to take the risk—of visiting—not *some* other place—but *the* Other Place."

"I don't follow you, Sir Alaric." And I wondered if I ought to clear out, although it was only just after nine. But I had to say something. "What's the difference between *some* other place and *the* other place?"

He giggled. I know that sounds all wrong for a little old fellow who must have been at least seventy-five; but you couldn't call it a laugh, and it wasn't hard enough for a cackle, and if it wasn't a giggle then I haven't a word for it. He got up now, and as he talked he began rummaging in a chest of drawers just behind his chair. "The Other Place—is round—a different kind of corner, Mr. Lindfield. You turn a corner—you didn't know was there. Something of a risk. But if you should decide—to pay it a visit—I'll be delighted—to oblige you." Evidently he'd found what he wanted, for now he turned quite sharply. There above the top of his chair were those ebony eyes, with no meaning in them that I could read, staring at me. "I will make it—simple for you—Mr. Lindfield. Yes—a door. You will go—to the Other Place—merely by opening a door. And there—you see, set in the bookshelves—is the door—you will use. Yes—that is the door. You still wish—to visit—the Other Place?"

"Why not?" I said, to humour him. I'd known one man who

had a lavatory in his library, behind a door covered with false book backs, and he had worked various gags with it. "What do I do?"

Now he showed me what he had taken out of the drawer. It was a shiny black piece of stone, rather like a large pebble. He sat down, leant forward, resting his elbows on his knees, and held out the stone. "It is simple. Look at this stone—stare into it—while you count—a hundred—quite slowly."

I stared at it and into it, and began counting. I could feel myself starting to squint. After I had counted twenty or so the surface of the stone turned into a hollow darkness that spread and spread as I kept on counting. I heard the grandfather clock chime quarter-past nine, but it seemed a long way off. By the time I had reached eighty my eyes ached and soon after that I began to feel dizzy.

"A hundred," I heard myself say out loud.

"Now, Mr. Lindfield," said Sir Alaric, who might have been telephoning from New Zealand, "get up—go straight to that door—open it—go through."

I felt cock-eyed as I marched towards the bookshelves, but I spotted the door at once and I'd sense enough left to realise it was similar to the one I'd seen before, covered with false book backs. As I opened it I thought I heard Sir Alaric telling me to enjoy my visit. Then I went through and closed the door behind me. I was in a narrow dark place, like a passage, lit at the end by three or four bars of gold. When I moved forward, I saw that these were bright streaks of sunlight coming through a rough broken sort of door on the right. I opened this door—and even now I can remember exactly how it creaked—and then I was staring, dazzled after the long gloom of Blackley, at a garden in full sunlight, in a high summer that looked as if it might go on for ever.

Now let's get one thing straight. It wasn't like a dream. All the dreams I've had have been patchy, with one sketchy sort of scene turning into another, as if there wasn't enough stuff around to make up even one solid background. And in a dream, I've found, you only notice what you want to notice, so to speak, and if a thing isn't in the centre of your focus then it just isn't there at all; there aren't a lot of things, as there are in real life, waiting to be properly noticed all round the edge of your consciousness. This garden wasn't like that at all. It was solidly there, with nothing unfinished and patchy about it. You knew it couldn't begin melting away, change into a room or a ship or a workshop. In fact, it seemed to have an extra solidity, as if it had stayed longer exactly like that than any ordinary garden could do.

A stone-flagged path went through a sort of tunnel of old-fashioned climbing roses. At the other end was a small lawn, bright in the sun, and beyond that some flower beds, burning with colour, set against a rough stone wall. When I reached the lawn I could just see the far bank of a river, not unlike the river at Hubberholme but broader and deeper. Beyond were fields rising sharply, then hanging woods and scree and rocks, and above them the hazy summits of high hills. It was a beautiful place, and you knew at once it was a long way from any trouble. And there was another thing, hard to describe. Have you ever known a room where there was a busy little clock, ticking your life away? And have you ever gone into that room when the clock wasn't there or had stopped, so that your life wasn't being ticked away? Well, arriving at this place was like that, only more so. The busy little clock inside you had stopped or wasn't there any more. The old *tick-tock-tick-tock-hurry-up-must-go* had gone. Nothing was wasting away, running down, draining out. I felt this at once, and it seemed to make everything sharper, more distinct, more itself and waiting to be noticed, whether it was the flame of the flowers or the blue of the sky.

I'd got some bearings now. The rough broken door I'd opened to let myself into this garden belonged to some sort of woodshed at the back of an inn. As I walked down the lawn I was coming round to the front of the inn, which was a longish low building with smooth walls washed in a faded pink. The lawn curved round there, losing its trim look, and became an outside drinking place. There were stout wooden tables and seats. A path led up to the open door of the inn. But I turned my back on that door and went to look over the bottom wall at the river. The nearer bank was quite close, with only a narrow strip of meadow, thick with buttercups and daisies, between it and the wall. A young man was fishing down there, and lying by his side, her head resting against him, was a dark young woman in a green dress. She caught sight of me, and as people do when they're feeling relaxed and happy, she gave me a smile and a wave of the arm that didn't mean anything in particular. And then I saw it was Mavis Gilbert.

Well, that didn't make any particular sense, but there was nothing wrong with it; and I was glad to see her there, looking so happy, complete—and that stuck out a mile—with the fellow she'd always been thinking about when I'd been with her. Good luck to them! I waved back; and then she made her chap turn round, and he waved too and made drinking motions before watching his rod again.

"It's about time too, Lindfield," somebody said, punching me in the back. That was Butterworth. Dawson was just coming out of the inn, carrying a tray with pots of beer on it. He gave a shout when he saw me; you'd have thought the two of them were the oldest friends I had, and had been waiting for me. They were dressed in old shirts and pants, and as brown and merry as sailors home from the sea. We drank the beer and then went loafing on the river bank, smoking and telling tales and watching the water slide by. No glass wall between us now—not on your life!

Their wives were around somewhere and afterwards I met them, all relaxed and friendly, not looking as if they were thinking about something else when they were talking to you. There were other people, of course, and some I'd met at Blackley, only they were quite different now, and others I hadn't, though I can't be sure. You said anything that came into your head, because anything that came into your head there was all right and not likely to hurt anybody; and so did the other people. It was a long day, not because it was dull but because there seemed time for everything, like summer days when you're a kid. And everybody there seemed a bit larger than life, not smaller as they do in places like Blackley. But I can't give you a proper idea of it. Don't think it was paradise or fairyland or anything fancy like that; it wasn't. But don't go too far the other way and think I was having something like a nice fine day at a holiday camp. It was out of this world all right, but it oughtn't to have been, if you see what I mean.

It wasn't until evening that I met her. She was the daughter of the genial fat old boy who kept the inn, and she'd been away from it all day. Her name was Paula, and she showed me the room I had to sleep in, at the end of the landing at the back. My bag was there too, though how it had got there God only knows. And I didn't care, all I cared about was Paula. She looked about thirty, and she was fairly tall for a woman but not scraggy, but broad and firmly set, and she'd a rather broad calm face, with darkish brown hair and grey eyes; and as soon as I saw her I knew I'd been looking for her all my life. There wasn't much light up in that bedroom then, for it was just after sunset and the hills overshadowed the back of the inn, and the room was settling into a green dusk that seemed to put us at the bottom of the sea. But there was light enough for me to see the look on her face, when she waited a moment after showing me the room. I guessed then she knew I felt as if I'd been looking for her all my life. You know that look of tender amusement women have when they're fond of you and sure of you too.

"All day I've been missing you," I said, though I couldn't have explained why I said it. "Everything's been grand, wonderful, just what I needed—except I've been missing you. Now you're here, Paula."

"Yes, Harvey," she said, as if she'd been giving me my first name for the last ten years. "Here I am."

I don't know whether she made a move or I did or we both

moved together, but then I had my arms round her—all so snug and easy that I might have done it ten thousand times before—and we kissed. And not one of those fighting, let's-get-on-with-it kisses neither; but one of the other sort you only find when everything else is dead right.

"And now I can't let you go," I told her.

But she pulled away gently, smiling at me. "You know you must. I'll be busy now until half-past ten. Come to me then—to my little sitting-room, through the green door at the far end of the kitchen—you remember? But not before half-past ten. You won't forget that, will you, Harvey?" And she looked at me anxiously, the only time she ever gave me that particular look.

I promised, and off she went then, a busy woman. Well, for the next hour or two, during supper and afterwards, when now and again she and I would exchange a look that was like a clasp of hands, everything was wonderful. It would have been good anyhow—the food and drink with friends so easy and happy, the jokes, the yarns, the songs and dancing after supper—but the idea of having her to myself later on raised everything another two thousand feet into the air. You know how you feel at those times, and this was a whole lot of those times rolled into one.

How long I'd have been there if I hadn't got impatient and turned nasty, I don't know; perhaps for ever. What got into me, what did the dirty on me, beats me, and you might say it's been beating me ever since. But when people began to move off, mostly two by two, and I didn't see her around inside, and the night outside, with no moon but a glitter of stars, was too big and lonely for me, I got impatient and didn't want to join in anything or talk to anybody, except to her of course, while the minutes went by like sick elephants. And I worked up some anger too, the way you do when you must have trouble. To hell with it! Why should she fix a time like that, as if everything had to be done her way? If I was good enough for her to see at half-past ten, I was good enough for quarter-past—what was the difference? I stuck it out a few minutes more, but all the time stoking my impatience like a furnace, and then made a dash for that green door at the far end of the kitchen, daring anybody to try and stop me.

Nobody did, of course; they never do when you're so hell-bent on trouble. There was the kitchen, empty and washed and swept out but still warm and heavy with the smell of food, and only a little lamp burning; but enough light to show me the green door at the opposite end. And now for Paula, who, if she didn't like it, because there were still ten minutes to go before the half-hour, could lump it—after all she belonged to me, and she knew it and knew I knew it. The green door opened easily—they always do, those doors—and there I was.

But not in any little sitting-room with Paula, of course. I was back in Sir Alaric's library, with my heart a lump of lead. I didn't even try to turn back, because I knew I hadn't a hope in hell. And I hated Sir Alaric and his library, which looked like a crummy old junk shop, and I hated myself.

I didn't want to look at Sir Alaric, so I looked at the grandfather clock. The time was nine-twenty; which meant that my day there had lasted about three minutes in here.

"Can I get back there?" I asked him.

"Not tonight, Mr. Lindfield." He seemed amused, and that didn't make me like him any better.

"Why not? I've only been out of this room for three minutes. And I didn't intend to come back so soon. That was a mistake."

"It always is. Perhaps—I ought—to have warned you. But I did—tell you—there was some risk——"

More in despair than hoping for anything, I went to that door and tore it open. There were shelves of odds and ends and a wash-hand basin in the cupboard. I thought I could hear Sir Alaric having a soft giggle. I felt like throwing the big paste-pot at him.

"I take it—Mr. Lindfield—that our little experiment—was successful. You arrived—at the Other Place—humph?"

"I arrived where I'd still like to be," I told him sourly.

"Then—clearly—it was the Other Place." He waited a moment. "You met—friends—there—humph?"

I made my reply a nod. Though he was responsible for getting me there, I didn't want to talk about it to him. But there was something else I had to talk about. "What's that black stone you asked me to stare at, Sir Alaric? And how does it do the trick?"

"It would be—just as sensible—to ask me—how the door—did the trick," he said reproachfully.

"Okay then, how did *you* do the trick?"

I don't know whether he was sleepy or just bored with me, but after he had shaken his head, to show me there was no reply coming, he began to yawn.

But I had to know *something*. "You said it was just a matter of getting round a corner, though of course a different kind of corner. More dimensions or something. Now—look, Sir Alaric, I don't want to keep bothering you, so tell me—could I do it for myself, sit in my hotel bedroom and get round that corner somehow?"

"You—could try, Mr. Lindfield." He sounded very cagey.

I couldn't leave it at that. "I suppose any door would do, wouldn't it, Sir Alaric?"

"Certainly. Any door."

"And that black polished stone was only something to stare at and concentrate on, wasn't it?"

"You—must have something—Mr. Lindfield—to stare at—certainly." Still cagey. And now he got up, and I knew the evening was over, even though it was only about half-past nine. Somehow my going to the Other Place—and I'd decided I might as well call it that—had finished things between us. Perhaps he felt that now he didn't owe me anything for saving him from that truck; we were quits. Perhaps he just didn't like me. I'd decided I didn't take to him, so all was fair and square between us.

"I seemed to be there about ten hours at least," I said, just to keep the conversation going. "But actually I was spending three minutes in that cupboard. That happens in dreams, of course. Yet this didn't seem like a dream."

"It wasn't."

"What was it then?"

He gave me another yawn. "Forgive me—Mr. Lindfield—sometimes I cannot sleep—but tonight—as you see——" In other words, Clear out, Lindfield.

There was more fog than rain that night, and the journey back to Blackley in the bus seemed very long and quite hopeless. At the end of it the Railway Hotel was waiting for me and was ready to do all it could to prove it was very different from the inn in the Other Place. I was in bed by about ten-forty-five and then spent the next four hours hearing railway wagons bumped and banged among the sidings. The following morning, Blackley looked darker and wetter and more dismal than ever.

Up at the Electrical Engineering Works that day I lost my temper because they hadn't yet completed a new bearing they'd promised me, and finally Butterworth was sent for, to explain the delay.

"And that's how it is, old man," he said, at the end of a long explanation, bristling with ministries and permits. "We keep asking them to get cracking, but if they won't move, there isn't a thing we can do. What's the matter? Don't you believe me?"

"Yes," I said, and then, taking a chance, went on: "But I was wondering what happened the other night—or was it last night?—after I left you and Dawson to go and see Paula."

"The other night? Paula?" Obviously he hadn't a clue.

There was no point in going on with it, but I had one more shot. "It was the same day you and I and Dawson drank beer in front of the inn and then went down to the river."

Butterworth had his share of brains but he was one of those Englishmen who never look as if they have any sense at all. He had a big moon-face made of underdone sirloin with some indeterminate features clustering together in the middle of it. And it looked so blank at that moment, I wanted to slug him. "I'm sorry, Lindfield old man," he said, "but there's some mistake."

"Yes, there is," I told him. "So please forget it. I was thinking of some other fellows. But do get that bearing in as soon as you can."

"We will, we will," he said, relieved to discover I'd returned to sanity. "Hate to keep you hanging about like this. Look here, old man, come out and dine with us tomorrow. There'll be eight of us—two tables of bridge."

Well, I went, and Dawson and his wife were there, and Mavis Gilbert; and even the other two, a couple called Jennings, I remembered having seen in the Other Place. So there we were, eight of us, and we'd all been in the Other Place, some of us spending hours together, living the life of Reilly. And although I hadn't much hope even then, I had to try them out. I started first with Mrs. Butterworth, who'd put me next to her at dinner. Did she, I asked, know a delightful little spot with an inn among the hills near a river; and I described the Other Place in some detail. I didn't even feel she was listening properly, because she was one of those anxious hostesses with half their minds in the kitchen; but when I'd finished and had felt a droning bore, she surprised me by saying: "No, I don't know that place. Where is it? Oh—you don't know." And then her eyes widened, and instead of being merely colourless, screwed-up and anxious they were blue, young and alive. "Mr. Lindfield, let's go and find it, shall we?" she whispered; and for a second she was almost the woman I had seen in the Other Place.

During a break in the bridge I was playing with them, I tried the Dawsons and Mrs. Jennings, concentrating on the inn this time, and telling them I had stayed there years ago and had now forgotten where it was. Dawson said it was in North Devon, his wife was sure that it was in Gloucestershire and had been pulled down, and Mrs. Jennings told us she knew a much nicer little pub in Dorset; and I knew that I had drawn a blank from the three of them. There wasn't a peep out of them to suggest they'd ever been near the Other Place. And what made it ten times worse was that I could still remember them there, which made this social evening of ours look as if we were playing charades about zombies.

We finished fairly early, so Mavis Gilbert, who was running me down town in her little car, suggested we stopped at her flat for a drink. When we'd tasted it and were feeling easy, she said: "Something's happened to you. I noticed it, and so did Mrs. Butterworth. What is it—or can't you tell?"

"I can tell some of it," I said, "but you won't know what I'm talking about. I saw you by a river—it was a bright warm morning—and you were wearing a green dress."

"Did I look nice?" she asked, smiling to show me she knew I was talking about a dream.

"You looked fine. Very happy too. You were with a fellow—I think I can describe him——"

"Go on. You must."

"He was a stiffish gingerish fellow with the greeny eyes his sort always have—and a scar on the left side of his face——"

"Rodney!" Then she was staring at me, white and angry. "I don't think that's funny. Somebody's been gossiping to you—and now you think this is an amusing way of telling me you know about Rodney and me. Well, I don't think it is."

"Look, Mavis, you've got it all wrong." I took her hand and wouldn't let her snatch it away. "I haven't been discussing you. I never heard of Rodney until now. I simply described the fellow I saw you with, when you were wearing a green dress, down by the river."

"What river?"

"I don't know what river. I wish I did," I told her. "There were lots of people there, the Butterworths and Dawsons included, and you were there with this fellow. There was also a girl called Paula—her father kept the inn where we were all staying." And I described Paula, trying to remember every detail of her appearance. "Do you know anybody like that?"

"She sounds rather like a girl I used to know called Norma Blake," said Mavis. "But she'd nothing to do with an inn. She went in for occupational therapy. It can't be the same girl. I can see this Paula was very special. But where was all this happening?"

So then I had to describe the inn and the river and the hills, and I gave her a sketch of what happened there. But I didn't explain about Sir Alaric and the black stone and the door.

"I don't know any place quite like that," she said slowly, looking rather foggy-eyed. "I was never anywhere like that with Rodney—worse luck! But do you mean to say you dreamt it all?" That's one thing about women, they take this sort of thing seriously, none of your "Come off it, old man" stuff about them.

But, even so, I didn't feel like telling her the whole story. "I can't explain," I said, "but I don't think I did dream it. Somehow I went there—I met all you people, happy as kings—I found Paula—and then, because I was in a hurry, I lost her. And all you people who were there don't seem to know what I'm talking about, which means either that you weren't there and I was making it all up or that you go there and then forget——"

"Oh—I can't bear that," she cried. "I wish you hadn't told me now. It's the sort of thing I've imagined—being some-where like that with Rodney—yes, night after night, here in this room, I've imagined it. And now you say you saw me there. You're making me feel miserable."

"I've made myself feel miserable. Let's change the subject."

"No," she said, "I must tell you about Rodney now."

And of course she did, with intervals for laughing and crying, and to her it was a wonderful heartbreaking story, enough to keep anybody on the edge of his seat, but to me, though I liked her and didn't mind what I'd seen of Rodney, it was nothing but two hours of trying to keep awake. I got back to the Railway Hotel, which didn't want to let me in, feeling rather worse than when I'd left it to enjoy this night out.

Well, the next few days were like walking across a wet

ploughed field wearing lead boots. I tried hard not to be sorry for myself—and about time, you'll say, and I agree; but when you're such a long way from home it's not so easy—and I went to the Reference Library to see if I could get a line on Sir Alaric's magic, and couldn't, and I also made some enquiries about Sir Alaric himself. But the people I asked either had never heard of him or knew he existed but weren't interested. Come to think of it, people in Blackley last winter didn't seem to be much interested in anything. They just went on living for something but didn't quite know what. Sometimes I felt they'd have been better off in the long run if they'd set fire to the place and then started all over again.

Then one night—as a matter of fact it was a Monday, and I think living through another Blackley Sunday might have had something to do with what happened—I had a few slugs of gin, because the whisky had given out, and told myself it was time for action. After all, Sir Alaric had shot me into the Other Place, and now he could shoot me there again, if only to stop me wandering round this grimy dump like a lost soul. He wasn't on the telephone, so I took a chance on his being in and caught a bus out there. It must have been one of the last, because it was late then for Blackley, round about ten o'clock. How I was to get back didn't worry me at all, not in the state of mind I was in then. And if Sir Alaric had gone to bed, I was ready to make such a commotion that he'd have to get up and let me in. I don't say I was plastered but I wasn't exactly sober.

But he hadn't gone to bed and he invited me in politely enough, though I didn't feel he was pleased to see me. He took me up to his library, where he'd been drowsing over the fire, and then he asked me, with no old-world courtesy at all, what I wanted. And obviously it was no use my pretending I'd gone there to enquire about his health, he'd spotted the mood I was in at once, so there was no point in trying to fool him.

"I want to get back to the Other Place," I told him. "And don't tell me to go away and try to go there on my own, because I've already tried and it doesn't work. Apart from that,

I'm having a bad time. I've talked to the people I met there—all except the most important one—and they don't know what I'm talking about. I've even tried putting the place out of my mind, but it won't stay out more than a few minutes. So now, Sir Alaric, with your help, I'm going back."

"Mr. Lindfield—you take—too much—for granted."

"That's because I'm a desperate man, Sir Alaric."

"Desperate men—Mr. Lindfield—should not attempt—to go anywhere. They should—stay at home—and begin to lose—their desperation."

"You're probably right, and we won't argue about it. In fact, we won't argue about anything. I'm going back there, Sir Alaric, and don't try to stop me. Where's that black stone?" And I got up and stood over him. I'm not proud of all this but I might as well tell you everything.

But if I thought I could frighten him, I was a mile out. All he did was to shake his head at me, as if I was ten years old. "You are behaving—very stupidly—Mr. Lindfield. You come here—uninvited—half drunk, I suspect——"

"About that, I'd say," I told him. "And you're quite right, I'm behaving badly. I've a lot of excuses but I won't bore you with them. Just bring out that black stone, Sir Alaric, and I'll do the rest. *Come on*," I shouted, when he hadn't made a move.

We stared at one another for what seemed quite a long time—and I thought I saw a flicker of flame in those black beady eyes of his—then he went to the chest of drawers and brought out the stone. This time he handed it to me instead of keeping it himself. "Do as you did before," he said coldly. "But be careful—to put down—the stone—before you go—to the door. If you will take—my advice—you will not—attempt this."

"I'm not taking your advice." And I began staring at the stone and counting up to a hundred. Everything happened just as it did the first time—the squinting, the hollow darkness that spread and spread, the dizziness. I put the stone down on the rug and went slowly over to the door in the bookshelves. I opened the door very carefully, as if something might break, probably because I was afraid the magic wouldn't have worked and that all I would see behind the door was the cupboard of odds and ends and its wash-hand basin. But no, I was back all right. There I was in that narrow dark passage with the streaks of sunlight at the end, coming through the rough broken door. Down I went, banged open the door, and hurried out into the garden, where I waited a moment, by the edge of the stone-flagged path among the roses, just to catch my breath.

I don't think I'm cheating when I tell you that even then, right at the start, I guessed something was wrong. But I'll admit I'm not sure what gave me the idea. Let me try and sort it out while you give yourself some more whisky. Okay, thanks, I'll join you. That's fine—thanks. Well, to begin with, everything I could see—and that wasn't much, remember— seemed narrower, not quite the right shape. And the sunshine had a kind of sting to it, wasn't mellow like the other sunshine I remembered. And then the time trick wasn't working right. I felt time had stopped, as it had done before, but it had stopped *in the wrong way*. Don't ask me just what I mean by that, because I'll be damned if I know. But it seemed to have stopped in a sinister way. Anyhow that's as near as I can get to what I felt.

I went through the tunnel of climbing roses and came out on to the lawn, and of course now I knew what to expect—the river, the hills, the drinking place in front of the inn itself. At a first glance, nothing had changed, except that I had an idea the colours were sharper and the shapes not quite the same, a bit meaner somehow. Like a copy of a picture that just missed it, if you see what I mean. And I didn't feel happy, not a bit.

Then it really got to work on me. That river, for instance. When I saw it out of the corner of my eye, not really paying attention to it, it looked just as it had done before, a full smooth stream. But as soon as I really looked at it, to take some pleasure in it, then it shrank to a mere trickle among cracked cakes of brown mud. So I'd look away, and at once

I'd know it was an easy broad stretch of water again. Another proper look, and it had dwindled again.

But the people were worse. As I stood there on the lawn, playing hide-and-seek with the river, I knew that where the tables and seats were, in front of the inn, to my left, people were drinking and talking and laughing, just as they'd done before. But when I turned that way, to shout "Hello!" and let them know I was there, they all froze up and were still as waxworks. And what put the finishing touch on it and gave me the creeps was that they were all looking at me, not with any particular expression on their faces but just looking, like dummies. I went towards them, half angry, half terrified. Not a sound. Not a move. Waxworks under an angry sun. I stopped, turned towards the river, and there it was, a miserable trickle again, while at the corner of my eye I could just catch a glimpse of the people coming to life again and could hear them talking and laughing. I whirled round on them, frantic now, and there they were, frozen, staring at me, silent as death.

"What the hell do you think you're playing at?" I shouted at them. Not a sound, not a quiver. And every goddam thing was wrong—the blue of the sky, the feel of the sun, the flowers that withered at a look. I felt I was outside time again, but out now on the wrong side. I had to make something happen in that place even if it meant being flattened by some giant dead hand that would drop from the sky.

I went charging through the gap in the stone wall to the staring dummies in the drinking place. The first one I reached was standing up and I saw that it was Jennings, who'd been dining with me at the Butterworth's.

"Now look, Jennings," I cried, putting a hand on his shoulder, "you know me—Lindfield." And now that I'd concentrated upon him the rest of them were all lively again, and Jennings was the only staring dummy there, unless you count me. "What's the idea? What's the matter with you people?"

He didn't say a thing, never gave so much as a twitch, and I felt that if I didn't take my hand off his shoulder I might push him over. So I took it away, but the next moment, in a blind fury because I couldn't get any response from him, I gave him a sharp slap across the cheek. And the next moment after that—and how it happened I can't tell you—I was down on the grass, out for the count, having taken the hardest punch I'd known since I'd boxed as a light-heavy for the University of Toronto. And while I was down there, waiting for the counting and the bell, I could hear, as if from far away, all those people talking and laughing over their drinks. Harvey Lindfield couldn't pay attention, so off they were again, enjoying themselves.

After a few minutes, feeling dazed and rather sick, I got on to my feet again and looked round. This time they weren't all completely frozen. They moved a little, like weeds under water, and they made some noise—but it wasn't a noise I was glad to hear, for they were laughing in a slow dim under-water fashion, and laughing at me. And then I wondered why I'd wasted any time on these people, if you could still call them people, when I didn't really care about them and had come back to find only one person—Paula. And I knew she wasn't out here. My only chance of finding her was somewhere inside the inn.

She was there, standing alone in the long room that was now as quiet and nearly as dark as a vault. She was no staring dummy but it might have been better if she had been, because the very sight of her standing there turned my heart into ice water. As I went up to her I saw that she was slowly shaking her head and that her cheeks were wet with tears. Everything that's ever been wrong between men and women, all the old long heartbreak, was there between us.

"Paula," I said, "I know it was my fault last time, but now I'm back and I came back, forced my way here, just because of you." I'd have gone on but I knew she wasn't going to talk to me, that she'd do nothing but shake her head and cry, the way they do when at last they feel it's hopeless.

Finally she moved away, and I followed her, wanting to say something but not knowing what to say. There was nobody else about; the place was empty, silent, a mile deep in misery. She went into the kitchen, which was cold and hadn't an appetising smell left, and she walked the length of it until she came to that green door. There she stopped long enough to give me a look and what might have been the shadow of a smile. The door was slowly closing behind her when I arrived—the big masterful type, God help me! I flung open that door and marched through like Alexander the Great.

But of course Sir Alaric wasn't impressed, and I don't blame him. I'd only been away a minute and a half this time, and he didn't care if I came out of his cupboard marching like Alexander the Great or crawling like the Hunchback of Notre Dame. All he cared about was getting me out of his house before I turned ugly and began kicking things around. So he told me in a hurry that a man who lived quarter of a mile down the road would run me into Blackley for about a pound. As a matter of fact he needn't have worried, because this last visit to the Other Place—if it was the Other Place—had taken all the fight out of me.

Once he had got me as far as his front door, Sir Alaric felt he could relax. "It was not—so pleasant—this time, Mr. Lindfield—humph?"

"It was very unpleasant," I told him grumpily. "But it probably serves me right for insisting upon going again. I've not behaved very well. But, come to that, neither have you."

"No, Mr. Lindfield," he said earnestly—and I can see him now, a little white-and-brown wisp of an old fellow, very English up to a point but with India or China looking out of his eyes, "you wrong me—as well as yourself. You have been—to the Other Place. Forget—this last visit—remember the first one. Now—of course—you are dissatisfied. But you have something—I imagine—to be dissatisfied about—now."

"I had before," I grumbled. "We all have. They're almost dying of it in Blackley. All you've done for me, in return for

not leaving you in front of that truck, is to add to my dissatisfaction."

"No," he said softly, "there is no addition. Not in—the long
run—I think. No—a subtraction. You will see."

Well, I don't know that I have seen, though now and again
I think I know what he meant. No, I never saw him again. I
called at his house again, a few nights later, but it was all shut
up and dark and then I was told he'd gone away, perhaps to
stand on his head in Bombay or turn a prayer wheel in Tibet.
I took that fellow Jennings out to lunch, just to see how he'd
react when I told him that a few nights before, in a place where
people turned into staring dummies when you looked hard at
them, he'd knocked me cold with a right hook I never even saw.
And of course he didn't react at all, just told me he'd stopped
dreaming now that he didn't eat cheese in the evening and
went on to say that British boxing or any other sport wasn't
what it had been.

I had a night out with Mavis Gilbert before I left Blackley,
and she told me more about Rodney and made me describe
Paula, though I left out the Other Place; and we got rather
tight and sentimental and tried to console one another with
some messy half-hearted love-making and were about as
clever at it as a couple of short-sighted bears. In fact the night
ended just as I'd imagined it would when I'd tried to avoid it.

Then the Blackley Electrical Engineering Company completed the machine to our specification, and after having it run
and testing it for a couple of days, I watched them take it down
and crate it and send it to Liverpool, ready for the next boat.
By this time my company was screaming for me, so I booked
a passage by plane, and on one of those muffled sad winter
afternoons I found myself at London Airport. I mention this
because it was there I saw Paula.

You know the way they shepherd you around in airports, as
if an idiot school was having a day's outing. Well, my lot was
being herded out to the plane just as another lot was being
herded in from one, so that a string of us passed each other.

And there was Paula—no question about it, I'd doubt my own name sooner.

"Paula!" I shouted, and hurried across to her.

She stopped but looked surprised, and not pleasantly surprised either. "There's some mistake," she said. "I'm Mrs. Endersly—and my name's not Paula and I don't know you."

"What's this?" And the big fellow behind her frowned at me. He owned her. He owned nearly everything. He was one of those men.

"Just a mistake, darling," she said to him, and then she gave me an apologetic little smile, probably because I was looking like a lost dog.

I don't know what I stammered at them, because what I'd suddenly seen in her eyes, like a sort of signal from miles away in their grey depths, had turned me upside down and inside out. And what it had seemed to say was something like this: *Yes, I was Paula when I was there, and now I remember you too, Harvey Lindfield, but where we were and what we can do about it, God knows!* And the next minute I was straggling along with the rest of the sheep, going towards the plane.

So here I am, back again at the first chance I had, but of course taking a holiday this time, with no more Blackley in the rain and the Railway Hotel. And I keep on describing the Other Place to people, and when they tell me they know something like it I go and have a look, which takes me to some of your nicest places, like this Hubberholme where we met this afternoon. Cornwall, Devon, Dorset, Cotswolds, Lake District—I've been all over. Oh—yes—I tried Sir Alaric again, but he died last February—somewhere abroad. Yes—and I asked about that black stone, but everything he had has been sold or given away, and nobody seems to know anything about it. I know—I might try to track it down, I've thought of that.

There's just one other thing worries me from time to time. You must have noticed this yourself. Now and again you meet people who look at you eagerly and cry "Haven't we met before somewhere?" And when you tell 'em you haven't, you see a light go out of their faces. Well, what worries me now about those people is that they may have been to some Other Place of their own and met me there, the way I did with those Blackley people—and of course with Paula. It's the damnedest thing, you know, if we all keep meeting in some Other Place and then can't make other people understand. My God!—look at the time. And I'm running up to Northumberland in the morning, because I've heard of a place there that might possibly be It—you never know, do you?

THE GREY ONES

"AND YOUR occupation, Mr. Patson?" Dr. Smith asked, holding his beautiful fountain pen a few inches from the paper.

"I'm an exporter," said Mr. Patson, smiling almost happily. Really this wasn't too bad at all. First, he had drawn Dr. Smith instead of his partner Dr. Meyenstein. Not that he had anything against Dr. Meyenstein, for he had never set eyes on him, but he had felt that it was at least a small piece of luck that Dr. Smith had been free to see him and Dr. Meyenstein hadn't. If he had to explain himself to a psychiatrist, then he would much rather have one simply and comfortingly called Smith. And Dr. Smith, a broad-faced man about fifty with giant rimless spectacles, had nothing forbidding about him, and looked as if he might have been an accountant, a lawyer or a dentist. His room too was reassuring, with nothing frightening in it; rather like a sitting-room in a superior hotel. And that fountain pen really was a beauty. Mr. Patson had already made a mental note to ask Dr. Smith where he had bought that pen. And surely a man who could make such a mental note, right off, couldn't have much wrong with him?

"It's a family business," Mr. Patson continued, smiling away. "My grandfather started it. Originally for the Far East. Firms abroad, especially in rather remote places, send us orders for all manner of goods, which we buy here on commission for them. It's not the business it was fifty years ago, of course, but on the other hand we've been helped to some extent by all these trade restrictions and systems of export licences, which people a long way off simply can't cope with. So we cope for them. Irritating work often, but not uninteresting. On the whole I enjoy it."

"That is the impression you've given me," said Dr. Smith,

making a note. "And you are reasonably prosperous, I gather? We all have our financial worries these days, of course. I know I have." He produced a mechanical sort of laugh, like an actor in a comedy that had been running too long, and Mr. Patson echoed him like another bored actor. Then Dr. Smith looked grave and pointed his pen at Mr. Patson as if he might shoot him with it. "So I think we can eliminate all that side, Mr. Patson—humph?"

"Oh yes—certainly—certainly," said Mr. Patson hurriedly, not smiling now.

"Well now," said Dr. Smith, poising his pen above the paper again, "tell me what's troubling you."

Mr. Patson hesitated. "Before I tell you the whole story, can I ask you a question?"

Dr. Smith frowned, as if his patient had made an improper suggestion. "If you think it might help——"

"Yes, I think it would," said Mr. Patson, "because I'd like to know roughly where you stand before I begin to explain." He waited a moment. "Dr. Smith, do you believe there's a kind of Evil Principle in the universe, a sort of super-devil, that is working hard to ruin humanity, and has its agents, who must really be minor devils or demons, living among us as people? Do you believe that?"

"Certainly not," replied Dr. Smith without any hesitation at all. "That's merely a superstitious fancy, for which there is no scientific evidence whatever. It's easy to understand—though we needn't go into all that now—why anybody, even today, suffering from emotional stress, might be possessed by such an absurd belief, but of course it's mere phantasy, entirely subjective in origin. And the notion that this Evil Principle could have its agents among us might be very dangerous indeed. It could produce very serious anti-social effects. You realise that, Mr. Patson?"

"Oh—yes—I do. I mean, at certain times when—well, when I've been able to look at it as you're looking at it, doctor. But most times I can't. And that, I suppose," Mr. Patson added, with a wan smile, "is why I'm here."

"Quite so," Dr. Smith murmured, making some notes. "And I think you have been well advised to ask for some psychiatric treatment. These things are apt to be sharply progressive, although their actual progress might be described as regressive. But I won't worry you with technicalities, Mr. Patson. I'll merely say that you—or was it Mrs. Patson?—or shall I say both of you?—are to be congratulated on taking this very sensible step in good time. And now you know, as you said, where I stand, perhaps you had better tell me all about it. Please don't omit anything for fear of appearing ridiculous. I can only help you if you are perfectly frank with me, Mr. Patson. I may ask a few questions, but their purpose will be to make your account clearer to me. By the way, here we don't adopt the psycho-analytic methods—we don't sit behind our patients while they relax on a couch—but if you would find it easier not to address me as you have been doing—face to face——"

"No, that's all right," said Mr. Patson, who was relieved to discover he would not have to lie on the couch and murmur at the opposite wall. "I think I can talk to you just like this. Anyhow, I'll try."

"Good! And remember, Mr. Patson, try to tell me everything relevant. Smoke if it will help you to concentrate."

"Thanks, I might later on." Mr. Patson waited a moment, surveying his memories as if they were some huge glittering sea, and then waded in. "It began about a year ago. I have a cousin who's a publisher, and one night he took me to dine at his club—the Burlington. He thought I might like to dine there because it's a club used a great deal by writers and painters and musicians and theatre people. Well, after dinner we played bridge for an hour or two, then we went down into the lounge for a final drink before leaving. My cousin was claimed by another publisher, so I was left alone for about quarter of an hour. It was then that I overheard Firbright—you know, the famous painter—who was obviously full of drink, although you couldn't exactly call him drunk, and was holding forth to a little group at the other side of the fireplace. Apparently he'd just come back from Syria or somewhere around there, and he'd picked this idea up from somebody there though he said it only confirmed what he'd been thinking himself for some time."

Dr. Smith gave Mr. Patson a thin smile. "You mean the idea of an Evil Principle working to ruin humanity?"

"Yes," said Mr. Patson. "Firbright said that the old notion of a scarlet-and-black sulphuric Satan, busy tempting people, was of course all wrong, though it might have been right at one time, perhaps in the Middle Ages. Then the devils were all fire and energy. Firbright quoted the poet Blake—I've read him since—to show that these weren't real devils and their Hell wasn't the real Hell. Blake, in fact, according to Firbright, was the first man here to suggest we didn't understand the Evil Principle, but in his time it had hardly made a start. It's during the last few years, Firbright said, that the horrible thing has really got to work on us."

"Got to work on us?" Dr. Smith raised his eyebrows. "Doing what?"

"The main object, I gathered from what Firbright said," Mr. Patson replied earnestly, "is to make mankind go the way the social insects went, to turn us into automatic creatures, mass beings without individuality, soulless machines of flesh and blood."

The doctor seemed amused. "And why should the Evil Principle want to do that?"

"To destroy the soul of humanity," said Mr. Patson, without an answering smile. "To eliminate certain states of mind that belong essentially to the Good. To wipe from the face of this earth all wonder, joy, deep feeling, the desire to create, to praise life. Mind you, that is what Firbright said."

"But you believed him?"

"I couldn't help feeling, even then, that there was something in it. I'd never thought on those lines before—I'm just a plain business man and not given to fancy speculation—but I had been feeling for some time that things were going wrong and that somehow they seemed to be out of our control. In theory I suppose we're responsible for the sort of lives we lead, but in actual practice we find ourselves living more and more the kind of life we don't like. It's as if," Mr. Patson continued rather wildly, avoiding the doctor's eye, "we were all compelled to send our washing to one huge sinister laundry, which returned everything with more and more colour bleached out of it until it was all a dismal grey."

"I take it," said Dr. Smith, "that you are now telling me what you thought and felt yourself, and not what you overheard this man Firbright say?"

"About the laundry—yes. And about things never going the right way. Yes, that's what I'd been feeling. As if the shape and colour and smell of things were going. Do you understand what I mean, doctor?"

"Oh—yes—it's part of a familiar pattern. Your age may have something to do with it——"

"I don't think so," said Mr. Patson sturdily. "This is something quite different. I've made all allowance for that."

"So far as you can, no doubt," said Dr. Smith smoothly, without any sign of resentment. "You must also remember that the English middle class, to which you obviously belong, has suffered recently from the effects of what has been virtually an economic and social revolution. Therefore any member of that class—and I am one myself—can't help feeling that life does not offer the same satisfactions as it used to do, before the War."

"Doctor Smith," cried Mr. Patson, looking straight at him now, "I know all about that—my wife and her friends have enough to say about it, never stop grumbling. But this is something else. I may tell you, I've always been a Liberal and believed in social reform. And if this was a case of one class getting a bit less, and another class getting a bit more, my profits going down and my clerk's and warehousemen's wages going up, I wouldn't lose an hour's sleep over it. But what I'm talking about is something quite different. Economics and politics and social changes may come into it, but *they're just being used.*"

"I don't follow you there, Mr. Patson."

"You will in a minute, doctor. I want to get back to what I overheard Firbright saying, that night. I got away from it just to make the point that I couldn't help feeling at once there was something in what he said. Just because for the first time somebody had given me a reason why these things were happening." He regarded the other man earnestly.

Smiling thinly, Dr. Smith shook his head. "The hypothesis of a mysterious but energetic Evil Principle, Mr. Patson, doesn't offer us much of a reason."

"It's a start," replied Mr. Patson, rather belligerently. "And of course that wasn't all, by any means. Now we come to these agents."

"Ah—yes—the agents." Dr. Smith looked very grave now. "It was Firbright who gave you that idea, was it?"

"Yes, it would never have occurred to me, I'll admit. But if this Evil Principle was trying to make something like insects out of us, it could do it in two ways. One—by a sort of remote control, perhaps by a sort of continuous radio programme, never leaving our minds alone, telling us not to attempt anything new, to play safe, not to have any illusions, to keep to routine, nor to waste time and energy wondering and brooding and being fanciful, and all that."

"Did Firbright suggest something of that sort was happening?"

"Yes, but it wasn't his own idea. The man he'd been talking about before I listened to him, somebody he'd met in the Near East, had told him definitely all that non-stop propaganda was going on. But the other way—direct control, you might call it—was by the use of these agents—a sort of Evil Fifth Column—with more and more of 'em everywhere, hard at work."

"Devils?" enquired the doctor, smiling. "Demons? What?"

"That's what they amount to," said Mr. Patson, not returning the smile but frowning a little. "Except that it gives one a wrong idea of them—horns and tails and that sort of thing. These are quite different, Firbright said. All you can definitely say is that they're not human. They don't belong to us. They don't like us. They're working against us. They have their orders. They know what they're doing. They work together in teams. They arrange to get jobs for one another, more and more influence and power. So what chance have we against them?" And Mr. Patson asked this question almost at the top of his voice.

"If such beings existed," Dr. Smith replied calmly, "we should soon be at their mercy, I agree. But then they don't exist—except of course as figures of phantasy, although in that capacity they can do a great deal of harm. I take it, Mr. Patson, that you have thought about—or shall we say *brooded over*—these demonic creatures rather a lot lately? Quite so. By the way, what do you call them? It might save time and possible confusion if we can give them a name."

"They're the Grey Ones," said Mr. Patson without any hesitation.

"Ah—the Grey Ones." Dr. Smith frowned again and pressed his thin lips together, perhaps to show his disapproval of such a prompt reply. "You seem very sure about this, Mr. Patson."

"Well, why shouldn't I be? You ask me what I call them, so I tell you. Of course I don't know what they call themselves. And I didn't invent that name for them."

"Oh—this is Firbright again, is it?"

"Yes, that's what I heard him calling them, and it seemed to me a very good name for them. They're trying to give everything a grey look, aren't they? And there's something essentially grey about these creatures themselves—none of your gaudy, red and black, Mephistopheles stuff about *them*. Just quiet grey fellows busy greying everything—that's them."

"Is it indeed? Now I want to be quite clear about this, Mr. Patson. As I suggested earlier, this idea of the so-called Grey

Ones is something I can't dismiss lightly, just because it might
have very serious anti-social effects. It is one thing to entertain
a highly fanciful belief in some mysterious Evil Principle
working on us for its own evil ends. It is quite another thing to
believe that actual fellow-citizens, probably highly conscientious and useful members of the community, are not human
beings at all but so many masquerading demons. You can see
that, can't you?"

"Of course I can," said Mr. Patson, with a flick of impatience. "I'm not stupid, even though I may have given you the
impression that I am. This idea of the Grey Ones—well, it
brings the whole thing home to you, doesn't it? Here they are,
busy as bees, round every corner, you might say."

The doctor smiled. "Yet you've never met one. Isn't that
highly suggestive? Doesn't that make you ask yourself what
truth there can be in this absurd notion? All these Grey Ones,
seeking power over us, influencing our lives, and yet you've
never actually come into contact with one. Now—now—Mr.
Patson——" And he wagged a finger.

"Who says I've never met one?" Mr. Patson demanded
indignantly. "Where did you get that idea from, doctor?"

"Do you mean to tell me——?"

"Certainly I mean to tell you. I know at least a dozen of 'em.
My own brother-in-law is one."

Dr. Smith looked neither shocked nor surprised. He merely
stared searchingly for a moment or two, then rapidly made
some notes. And now he stopped sounding like a rather playful
schoolmaster and became a doctor in charge of a difficult case.
"So that's how it is, Mr. Patson. You know at least a dozen Grey
Ones, and one of them is your brother-in-law. That's correct,
isn't it? Good! Very well, let us begin with your brother-in-law.
When and how did you make the discovery that he is a Grey
One?"

"Well, I'd wondered about Harold for years," said Mr.
Patson slowly. "I'd always disliked him but I never quite knew
why. He'd always puzzled me too. He's one of those chaps

who don't seem to have any centre you can understand. They don't act from any ordinary human feeling. They haven't motives you can appreciate. It's as if there was nothing inside 'em. They seem to tick over like automatic machines. Do you know what I mean, doctor?"

"It would be better now if you left me out of it. Just tell me what you thought and felt—about Harold, for instance."

"Yes, Harold. Well, he was one of them. No centre, no feeling, no motives. I'd try to get closer to him, just for my wife's sake, although they'd never been close. I'd talk to him at home, after dinner, and sometimes I'd take him out. You couldn't call him unfriendly—that at least would have been *something*. He'd listen, up to a point, while I talked. If I asked him a question, he'd make some sort of reply. He'd talk himself in a kind of fashion, rather like a leading article in one of the more cautious newspapers. Chilly stuff, grey stuff. Nothing exactly wrong with it, but nothing right about it either. And after a time, about half an hour or so, I'd find it hard to talk to him, even about my own affairs. I'd begin wondering what to say next. There'd be a sort of vacuum between us. He had a trick, which I've often met elsewhere, of deliberately not encouraging you to go on, of just staring, waiting for you to say something silly. Now I put this down to his being a public official. When I first knew him, he was one of the assistants to the Clerk of our local Borough Council. Now he's the Clerk, quite a good job, for ours is a big borough. Well, a man in that position has to be more careful than somebody like me has. He can't let himself go, has too many people to please—or rather, not to offend. And one thing was certain about Harold—and that ought to have made him more human, but somehow it didn't—and that was that he meant to get on. He had ambition, but there again it wasn't an ordinary human ambition, with a bit of fire and nonsense in it somewhere, but a sort of cold determination to keep on moving up. You see what I mean? Oh—I forgot—no questions. Well, that's how he was—and is. But then I noticed another thing about Harold.

And even my wife had to agree about this. He was what we called a damper. If you took him out to enjoy something, not only didn't he enjoy it himself but he contrived somehow to stop you enjoying it. I'm very fond of a good show—and don't mind seeing a really good one several times—but if I took Harold along then it didn't matter what it was, I couldn't enjoy it. He wouldn't openly attack it or sneer at it, but somehow by just being there, sitting beside you, he'd cut it down and take all the colour and fun out of it. You'd wonder why you'd wasted your evening and your money on such stuff. It was the same if you tried him with a football or cricket match, you'd have a boring afternoon. And if you asked him to a little party, it was fatal. He'd be polite, quite helpful, do whatever you asked him to do, but the party would never get going. It would be just as if he was invisibly spraying us with some devilish composition that made us all feel tired and bored and depressed. Once we were silly enough to take him on a holiday with us, motoring through France and Italy. It was the worst holiday we ever had. He killed it stone dead. Everything he looked at seemed smaller and duller and greyer than it ought to have been. Chartres, the Loire country, Provence, the Italian Riviera, Florence, Siena—they were all cut down and greyed over, so that we wondered why we'd ever bothered to arrange such a trip and hadn't stuck to Torquay and Bournemouth. Then, before I'd learnt more sense, I'd talk to him about various plans I had for improving the business, but as soon as I'd described any scheme to Harold I could feel my enthusiasm ebbing away. I felt—or he made me feel—any possible development wasn't worth the risk. Better stick to the old routine. I think I'd have been done for now if I hadn't had sense enough to stop talking to Harold about the business. If he asked me about any new plans, I'd tell him I hadn't any. Now all this was long before I knew about the Grey Ones. But I had Harold on my mind, particularly as he lived and worked so close to us. When he became Clerk to the Council, I began to take more interest in our municipal affairs, just to see what influence Harold was having on them. I made almost a detective job of it. For instance, we'd had a go-ahead, youngish Chief Education Officer, but he left and in his place a dull timid fellow was appointed. And I found out that Harold had worked that. Then we had a lively chap as Entertainments Officer, who'd brightened things up a bit, but Harold got rid of him too. Between them, he and his friend, the Treasurer, who was another of them, managed to put an end to everything that added a little colour and sparkle to life round our way. Of course they always had a good excuse—economy and all that. But I noticed that Harold and the Treasurer only made economies in one direction, on what you might call the anti-grey side, and never stirred themselves to save money in other directions, in what was heavily official, pompous, interfering, irritating, depressing, calculated to make you lose heart. And you must have noticed yourself that we never do save money in those directions, either in municipal or national affairs, and that what I complained of in our borough was going on all over the country—yes, and as far as I can make out, in a lot of other countries too."

Dr. Smith waited a moment or two, and then said rather sharply: "Please continue, Mr. Patson. If I wish to make a comment or ask a question, I will do so."

"That's what I meant earlier," said Mr. Patson, "when I talked about economics and politics and social changes just being used. I've felt all the time there was something behind 'em. If we're doing it for ourselves, it doesn't make sense. But the answer is of course that we're not doing it for ourselves, we're just being manipulated. Take Communism. The Grey Ones must have almost finished the job in some of those countries—they hardly need to bother any more. All right, we don't like Communism. We must make every possible effort to be ready to fight it. So what happens? More and more of the Grey Ones take over. This is their chance. So either way they win and we lose. We're further along the road we never wanted to travel. Nearer the bees, ants, termites. Because we're being pushed. My God—doctor—can't you feel it yourself?"

"No, I can't, but never mind about me. And don't become too general, please. What about your brother-in-law, Harold? When did you decide he was a Grey One?"

"As soon as I began thinking over what Firbright said," replied Mr. Patson. "I'd never been able to explain Harold before—and God knows I'd tried often enough. Then I saw at once he was a Grey One. He wasn't born one, of course, for that couldn't possibly be how it works. My guess is that sometime while he was still young, the soul or essence of the real Harold Sothers was drawn out and a Grey One slipped in. That must be going on all the time now, there are so many of them about. Of course they recognise each other and help each other, which makes it easy for them to handle us humans. They know exactly what they're up to. They receive and give orders. It's like having a whole well-disciplined secret army working against us. And our only possible chance now is to bring 'em out into the open and declare war on 'em."

"How can we do that," asked Dr. Smith, smiling a little, "if they're secret?"

"I've thought a lot about that," said Mr. Patson earnestly, "and it's not so completely hopeless as you might think. After a time you begin to recognise a few. Harold, for instance. And our Borough Treasurer. I'm certain he's one. Then, as I told you at first, there are about a dozen more that I'd willingly stake a bet on. Yes, I know what you're wondering, doctor. If they're all officials, eh? Well no, they aren't, though seven or eight of 'em are—and you can see why—because that's where the power is now. Another two are up-and-coming politicians—and not in the same Party neither. One's a banker I know in the City—and he's a Grey One all right. I wouldn't have been able to spot them if I hadn't spent so much time either with Harold or wondering about him. They all have the same cutting-down and bleaching stare, the same dead touch. Wait till you see a whole lot of 'em together, holding a conference." Then Mr. Patson broke off abruptly, as if he felt he had said too much.

Dr. Smith raised his eyebrows so that they appeared above his spectacles, not unlike hairy caterpillars on the move. "Perhaps you would like a cigarette now, Mr. Patson. No, take one of these. I'm no smoker myself but I'm told they're excellent. Ah—you have a light. Good! Now take it easy for a minute or two because I think you're tiring a little. And it's very important you should be able to finish your account of these—er—Grey Ones, if possible without any hysterical over-emphasis. No, no—Mr. Patson—I didn't mean to suggest there'd been any such over-emphasis so far. You've done very well indeed up to now, bearing in mind the circumstances. And it's a heavy sort of day, isn't it? We seem to have too many days like this, don't we? Or is it simply that we're not getting any younger?" He produced his long-run actor's laugh. Then he brought his large white hands together, contrived to make his lips smile without taking the hard stare out of his eyes, and said finally: "Now then, Mr. Patson. At the point you broke off your story, shall we call it, you had suggested that you had seen a whole lot of Grey Ones together, holding a conference. I think you might very usefully enlarge that rather astonishing suggestion, don't you?"

Mr. Patson looked and sounded troubled. "I'd just as soon leave that, if you don't mind, doctor. You see, if it's all nonsense, then there's no point in my telling you about that business. If it isn't all nonsense——"

"Yes," said Dr. Smith, after a moment, prompting him, "if it isn't all nonsense——?"

"Then I might be saying too much." And Mr. Patson looked about for an ashtray as if to hide his embarrassment.

"There—at your elbow, Mr. Patson. Now please look at me. And remember what I said earlier. I am not interested in fanciful theories of the universe or wildly imaginative interpretations of present world conditions. All I'm concerned with here, in my professional capacity, is your state of mind, Mr. Patson. That being the case, it's clearly absurd to suggest that you might be saying too much. Unless you are perfectly frank with me, it will be very difficult for me to help you. Come now, we agreed about that. So far you've followed my instructions admirably. All I ask now is for a little more cooperation. Did you actually attend what you believed to be a conference of these Grey Ones?"

"Yes, I did," said Mr. Patson, not without some reluctance. "But I'll admit I can't prove anything. The important part may be something I imagined. But if you insist, I'll tell you what happened. I overheard Harold and our Borough Treasurer arranging to travel together to Maundby Hall, which is about fifteen miles north of where I live. I'd never been there myself but I'd heard of it in connection with various summer schools and conferences and that sort of thing. Perhaps you know it, Dr. Smith?"

"As a matter of fact, I do. I had to give a paper there one Saturday night. It's a rambling Early Victorian mansion, with a large ballroom that's used for the more important meetings."

"That's the place. Well, it seems they were going there to attend a conference of the New Era Community Planning Association. And when I overheard them saying that, first I told myself how lucky I was not to be going too. Then afterwards, thinking it over, I saw that if you wanted to hold a meeting that no outsider in his senses would want to attend, you couldn't do better than hold it in a country house that's not too easy to get at, and call it a meeting or conference of the New Era Community Planning Association. I know if anybody said to me 'Come along with me and spend the day listening to the New Era Community Planning Association', I'd make any excuse to keep away. Of course it's true that anybody like Harold couldn't be bored. The Grey Ones are never bored, which is one reason why they are able to collar and hold down so many jobs nowadays, the sort of jobs that reek of boredom. Well, this New Era Community Planning Association might be no more than one of the usual societies of busybodies, cranks and windbags. But then again it might be something very different, and I kept thinking about it in connection with the Grey Ones. Saturday was the day of the conference. I went down to my office in the morning, just to go through the post and see if there was anything urgent, and then went home to lunch. In the middle of the afternoon I felt I had to know what was happening out at Maundby Hall, so off I went in my car. I parked it just outside the grounds, scouted round a bit, then found an entrance through a little wood at the back. There was nobody about, and I sneaked into the house by way of a servants' door near the pantries and larders. There were some catering people around there, but nobody bothered me. I went up some back stairs and after more scouting, which I enjoyed as much as anything I've done this year, I was guided by the sound of voices to a small door in a corridor upstairs. This door was locked on the inside, but a fellow had once shown me how to deal with a locked door when the key's still in the lock on the other side. You slide some paper under the door, poke the key out so that it falls on to the paper and then slide the paper back with the key on it. Well, this trick worked and I was able to open the door, which I did very cautiously. It led to a little balcony overlooking the floor of the ballroom. There was no window near this balcony so that it was rather dark up there and I was able to creep down to the front rail without being seen. There must have been between three and four hundred of them in that ballroom, sitting on little chairs. This balcony was high above the plat-form, so I had a pretty good view of them as they sat facing it. They looked like Grey Ones, but of course I couldn't be sure. And for the first hour or so, I couldn't be sure whether this really was a meeting of the New Era Community Planning Association or a secret conference of Grey Ones. The stuff they talked would have done for either. That's where the Grey Ones are so damnably clever. They've only to carry on doing what everybody expects them to do, in their capacity as sound conscientious citizens and men in authority, to keep going with their own hellish task. So there I was, getting cramp, no wiser. Another lot of earnest busybodies might be suggesting new ways of robbing us of our individuality. Or an organised covey of masquerading devils and demons might be making plans to bring us nearer to the insects, to rob us of our souls. Well, I was just about to creep back up to the corridor, giving it up as a bad job, when something happened." He stopped, and looked dubiously at his listener.

"Yes, Mr. Patson," said Dr. Smith encouragingly, "then something happened?"

"This is the part you can say I imagined, and I can't prove I didn't. But I certainly didn't dream it, because I was far too cramped and aching to fall asleep. Well, the first thing I noticed was a sudden change in the atmosphere of the meeting. It was as if somebody very important had arrived, although I didn't see anybody arriving. And I got the impression that the *real* meeting was about to begin. Another thing—I knew for certain now that this was no random collection of busybodies and windbags, that they were all Grey Ones. If you asked me to tell you in detail how I knew, I couldn't begin. But I noticed something else, after a minute or two. These Grey Ones massed together down there had now a positive quality of their own, which I'd never discovered before. It wasn't that they were just negative, not human, as they were at ordinary times; they had this positive quality, which I can't describe except as a sort of chilly hellishness. As if they'd stopped pretending to be human and were letting themselves go, recovering their demon natures. And here I'm warning you, doctor, that my account of what happened from then is bound to be sketchy and peculiar. For one thing, I wasn't really well placed up in that balcony, not daring to show myself and only getting hurried glimpses; and for another thing, I was frightened. Yes, doctor, absolutely terrified. I was crouching there just above three or four hundred creatures from some cold hell. That quality I mentioned, that chilly hellishness, seemed to come rolling over me in waves. I might have been kneeling on the edge of a pit of iniquity a million miles deep. I felt the force of this hellishness not on the outside but inside, as if the very essence of me was being challenged and attacked. One slip, a black-out, and then I might waken up to find myself running a concentration camp, choosing skins for lampshades. Then somebody, something, arrived. Whoever or whatever they'd been waiting for was down there on the platform. I knew that definitely. But I couldn't see him or it. All I could make out was a sort of thickening and whirling of the air down there. Then out of that a voice spoke, the voice of the leader they had been expecting. But this voice didn't come from outside, through my ears. It spoke inside me, right in the centre, so that it came out to my attention, if you see what I mean. Rather like a small, very clear voice on a good telephone line, but coming from inside. I'll tell you frankly I didn't want to stay there and listen, no matter what big secrets were coming out; all I wanted to do was to get away from there as soon as I could; but for a few minutes I was too frightened to make the necessary moves."

"Then you heard what this—er—voice was saying, Mr. Patson?" the doctor asked.

"Some of it—yes."

"Excellent! Now this is important." And Dr. Smith pointed his beautiful fountain pen at Mr. Patson's left eye. "Did you learn from it anything you hadn't known before? Please answer me carefully."

"I'll tell you one thing you won't believe," cried Mr. Patson. "Not about the voice—we'll come to that—but about those Grey Ones. I risked a peep while the voice was talking, and what I saw nearly made me pass out. There they were—three or four hundred of 'em—not looking human at all, not making any attempt; they'd all gone back to their original shapes. They looked—this is the nearest I can get to it—like big semi-transparent toads—and their eyes were like six hundred electric lamps burning under water, all greeny, unblinking, and shining out of Hell."

"But what did you hear the voice say?" Dr. Smith was urgent now. "How much can you remember? That's what I want to know. Come along, man."

Mr. Patson passed a hand across his forehead and then looked at the edge of this hand with some astonishment, as if he had not known it would be so wet. "I heard it thank them in the name of Adaragraffa—Lord of the Creeping Hosts. Yes, I could have imagined it—only I never knew I'd that sort of imagination. And what is imagination anyhow?"

"What else—what else—did you hear, man?"

"Ten thousand more were to be drafted into the Western Region. There would be promotions for some there who'd been on continuous duty longest. There was to be a swing over from the assault by way of social conditions, which could almost look after itself now, to the draining away of character, especially in the young of the doomed species. Yes, those were the very words," Mr. Patson shouted, jumping and up waving his arms. "Especially in the young of the doomed species. Us—d'you understand—us. And I tell you—we haven't a chance unless we start fighting back now—*now*—yes, and with everything we've got left. Grey Ones. And more and more of them coming, taking charge of us, giving us a push here, a shove there—down—down—down——"

Mr. Patson found his arms strongly seized and held by the doctor, who was clearly a man of some strength. The next moment he was being lowered into his chair. "Mr. Patson," said the doctor sternly, "you must not excite yourself in this fashion. I cannot allow it. Now I must ask you to keep still and quiet for a minute while I speak to my partner, Dr. Meyenstein. It's for your own good. Now give me your promise."

"All right, but don't be long," said Mr. Patson, who suddenly felt quite exhausted. As he watched the doctor go out, he wondered if he had not said either too much or not enough. Too much, he felt, if he was to be accepted as a sensible business man who happened to be troubled by some neurotic fancies. Not enough, perhaps, to justify, in view of the doctor's obvious scepticism, the terrible shaking excitement that had possessed him at the end of their interview. No doubt, round the corner, Doctors Smith and Meyenstein were having a good laugh over this rubbish about Grey Ones. Well, they could try and make him laugh too. He would be only too delighted to join them, if they could persuade him he had been deceiving himself. Probably that is what they would do now.

"Well, Mr. Patson," said Dr. Smith, at once brisk and grave, as he returned with two other men, one of them Dr. Meyenstein and the other a bulky fellow in white who might be a male nurse. All three moved forward slowly as Dr. Smith spoke to him. "You must realise that you are a very sick man—sick in mind if not yet sick in body. So you must put yourself in our hands."

Even as he nodded in vague agreement, Mr. Patson saw what he ought to have guessed before, that Dr. Smith was a Grey One and that now he had brought two more Grey Ones with him. There was a fraction of a moment, as the three of them bore down upon him to silence his warning for ever, when he thought he caught another glimpse of the creatures in the ballroom, three of them now like big semi-transparent toads, six eyes like electric lamps burning under water, all greeny, unblinking, shining triumphantly out of Hell. . . .

UNCLE PHIL ON TV

UNCLE PHIL'S insurance money came to a hundred and fifty pounds, so that night the Grigsons had a family conference about it, in the big front room above the shop. They were all there—Mum and Dad, Ernest, Una and George her husband (Fleming was their name, but of course Una was a Grigson and George helped Dad in the shop), and even Joyce and young Steve, who were usually off and out and stayed out, as Mum said, till all hours. As a matter of fact Mum, who had let herself cool down and had tidied her hair for once, looked very proud and happy to see them all together like that, just as if it was Christmas though it was only October and her feet weren't so bad as they always were at Christmas. It was nice, even though Uncle Phil had been Mum's elder brother and now he was dead and this hundred and fifty pounds was his insurance.

"It's mine by rights of course," said Mum, referring to the money, "but I think—and so does Dad—it ought to be spent on something for the family."

"Had him to keep," said Dad darkly, "and had to put up with him."

"I'll say," cried young Steve.

"You be quiet," said Mum. "I won't say you hadn't to put up with him, but he did pay his share——"

"Not lately he didn't," said Dad. "Worked out all right at first, when prices weren't so bad, but not lately it didn't. Not at twenty-three shillings a week."

"That's right," said Ernest, who was a railway clerk and very steady, so steady that sometimes he hardly seemed alive at all. "Some of us had him to keep. I'm not saying we oughtn't to have. I'm just making the point, that's all."

"I wish somebody'd come to the point," cried Joyce, who of course wanted to be off again. "If there *is* one."

"That'll do, you saucy monkey," said Mum, who soon lost her temper with Joyce. "Just remember this was Uncle Phil's money in a way. And now he's Passed On." And then she could have bit her tongue off, saying a silly thing like that. For now a shadow settled over the family gathering.

The doctor, an impatient and over-worked man, had been very angry about Uncle Phil's passing on, which ought not to have happened when it did. Uncle Phil had had a very bad heart, and the doctor had warned Mum and Dad that the things Uncle Phil had to take, when he felt an attack coming on, had to be within easy reach. But that Tuesday morning somebody had put Uncle Phil's box of things up on the mantelpiece, where he couldn't reach them when his last fatal attack had come on. A lot of questions had been asked, of course, but nobody could remember putting it up there; and it had been all very awkward and even downright nasty. It hadn't been done on purpose, even the doctor didn't suggest that, but somebody in the family had been very careless. And there was no getting away from the fact that for various good reasons they were all glad, or at least relieved, that Uncle Phil was no longer with them. He hadn't liked them any more than they'd liked him. Even Mum had never been really fond of him. Dad had tried to put up with him, you couldn't say more than that. And the younger members of the family had always disliked and feared the sarcastic old man, with his long sharp nose and sharper tongue, his slow movements, his determined refusal to leave the fireside even when they were entertaining friends and hated to have him there watching them. Before he had come to them, he had worked for some Loan Company, nothing but moneylenders really, in Birmingham, and perhaps this job had made him very hard and cynical, you might say nasty-minded. Also, some accident he'd had made him carry his head on one side, so that he always looked as if he was trying to see round a corner; and even this, to say nothing of the rest of him, got on their nerves. So naturally it was a relief to know that never again would they see him coming in to dinner, so deliberate and slow, his head on one side, his long nose seeming to sniff at them and their doings, a hard old man all ready to make some cutting remark. But at the same time it was awkward because of those things that were up on the mantelpiece when they ought to have been on the little table by his chair. So while Mum was telling herself what a daft donkey she'd been, everybody else was silent.

Then Mum for once was glad George Fleming was such a brassy sort of chap. "Here, we've had the funeral once, we don't want it again," cried George. "He's gone, and that's that. And I'm not going to pretend I'm sorry. He never liked me and I never liked him. If you ask me, he looked like a pain in the neck, and he was one——"

"Every time, George," young Steve shouted.

"I couldn't agree more," cried Joyce, who picked up a lot of fancy talk at work even if she didn't pick up much money there.

"Let me finish," said George, frowning at the young Grigsons, for whom he was more than a match. "You've got this hundred and fifty quid, Ma. And you don't know what to do with it—right? Well, I got an idea. Something we could all enjoy."

This was more like it. Mum gave him an encouraging smile. "And what would that be, George?"

"Television set," replied George, looking round in triumph.

Then everybody began talking at once, but George, who didn't look like a bull for nothing, managed to shout them down. "Now listen, listen! We've got TV here in Smallbridge at last, and comes over good too. What more d'you want? Gives you everything. Sport for me and Dad and Steve. Plays and games and all that for you women. Dancing and fashion shows too. Variety turns we'd all like. Serious stuff for Ernest. Ask your friends in to enjoy it."

That was what clinched it for Mum, who had several

friends who certainly wouldn't be able to afford a set of their own for some time; she saw herself bringing them in and telling them what was in store. So she made herself heard above the babble that broke out again. "What would a nice set cost, George?"

"You could get a beauty," replied George, who always knew the price of everything, "for a hundred and twenty quid. Saw one at Stocks's the other day. Might get a bit of discount from Alf Stocks too."

Dad and Ernest nodded a grave assent to this. Una, who wouldn't have dared do anything else, supported her husband. Joyce hinted that a home with a good television set might be more popular with herself and girl and boy friends. Young Steve was all for it, of course. So it was agreed that George should take advantage of the first slack half-hour in the shop the next day and go along to Stocks's to bargain for the hundred-and-twenty-pound beauty. Then there was much excited happy talk about TV programmes and who could be asked in to see them and who couldn't; and clearly there was a general feeling, although even George dared not openly express it, that fate had been kind in exchanging Uncle Phil, whom nobody wanted, for this new wonder of the world.

Two days later, before Dad and George had come up from the shop and the others had returned from work, the television set, with aerial and everything in order, was there in the front sitting-room, looking a beauty indeed. Alf Stocks himself showed Mum and Una how to work it, and wouldn't leave until he'd seen each of them turn it on and off properly, which took some time because Mum was flustered. As soon as Alf Stocks had gone, Mum and Una looked at one another, and though it was nearly time to be getting a meal ready for Joyce and the men, they decided to have a look by themselves for ten minutes or so. Una turned it on, not having any trouble at all, and it began showing them a film that looked like an oldish cowboy film, which wasn't exactly their style, still it was wonderful having it in the sitting-room like that. The people were small and not always easy to see and their voices were loud enough for giants, which made it a bit confusing; but they watched it for quarter of an hour, and then Mum said they'd have to be getting the meal ready or there'd be trouble. Una wanted to keep it on, but Mum said that would be wasting it. So they turned it off, just after the Sheriff had been getting some evidence about the rustlers from Drywash Peter the Old-timer.

They didn't say anything for a minute or two, while Una was starting to lay the table and Mum began doing the haddock. Then Mum popped out of the kitchen, and looked at Una as if she had something rather important to say but didn't know how to start. And Una looked at her too, not saying anything either. Then finally Mum said: "Una, did you happen to notice that other little man who was there—you know in that last bit we saw—with the Sheriff?"

"What about him?" asked Una, who had now started cutting bread.

"Well, did you notice anything?"

"Seeing that you're asking—I did." But she went on cutting bread.

"What, then?"

"I thought, just for a sec," said Una, sawing away at the loaf and sounding very calm, "he looked just like Uncle Phil. Is that what you mean?"

"Yes it is," said Mum, "and it gave me quite a turn."

"Just a what's-it—coincidence," said Una. "There—that ought to do."

"Plenty," said Mum. "It's only getting stale if you cut too much. There's some of that sponge in the tin. I'll get it. Yes, of course—as you say—just a coincidence. Nearly made me catch my breath, though. I wouldn't say anything to the others, Una. They'd only laugh."

"George included. And then he'd tell me he'd had quite enough of Uncle Phil. So I won't say anything." Una waited a moment. "Who you having in tonight to look at it?"

"We'll settle that when they all come in," replied Mum rather proudly.

There was a bit of trouble, as Mum guessed there would be, when they all did come in. Joyce and Steve, with some timid backing by Una, were in favour of what amounted to a continuous performance by the set. Dad and Ernest were dead against this idea, which they thought wasteful and silly. They wanted to make a sort of theatre of it, with everybody sitting in position a few minutes before the chosen programme was ready to start, and then lights turned off and *Quiet, please!* and all that. George Fleming thought that was going too far but he was against the continuous touch too. One thing they had to decide, he pointed out, was how many people could sit in comfort and see the set properly. So he and Steve went and worked it out and after some argument agreed that you could manage a dozen, that is, if you brought up the old settee as a sort of dress circle. Meanwhile an argument had broken out among the women about who ought to be invited for this first evening, until Dad, with some moral support from Ernest, put his foot down, as he said, and declared that tonight it would be family only. Ernest, who was inclined to look on the dark side, said they needed at least one evening of it to make sure the set worked properly and didn't make them look silly.

Mum had been disappointed at first but after they had washed up and tidied, and Joyce, staying in for once, and Steve had arranged the chairs in front of the set, she felt it was nice and cosy to have a television show just for themselves. George, who had had a technical session with Alf Stocks in the shop, took charge of the set in his masterful way, so that Dad, who had a bit too much of George at times, whispered to Mum that they ought not to have let him buy the set for them, because now you'd think he owned it. However, there they all were, Dad and Ernest with their pipes going, Una and Joyce eating toffee-de-luxe, and the set winking brightly at them. There was some argument about how much light there ought to be in the room, and this was settled finally by switching off the bowl lamps in the centre and leaving on the standard on the other side. Then the television picture looked bright, sharp and lovely.

The first item, dullish for the Grigsons, was about how men trained for various sports. Mum and Una were bored with it until near the end, when there was a scene of boxers in a gymnasium. Not that they cared about that of course, but the point was that some men who weren't boxers appeared in this scene, carrying things about or just looking in, and among these men—just seen in a flash, that's all—was a little elderly man who carried his head to one side and seemed to have a long nose. Steve, who was always quick, spotted him and sang out that a little chap had just gone past who looked like old Uncle Phil. The others didn't notice or didn't bother to say anything; but Mum and Una gave each other a look, and, as they said afterwards, felt quite peculiar, because, after all, this was the second time.

Well, next was a snooty lady talking about clothes, with some models helping her, and of course this was all right because no men came into it at all. But the only one who liked it much was Joyce, who thought about nothing but clothes and boys. However, it didn't last long.

Then—and this was when the bother really started—there was a sort of game, about telling where you were born, a very popular programme that had had a lot of write-ups in the papers. A lovely actress was in it, as well as that man who was always in these shows just because at any minute he might be very rude and have to apologise afterwards. But there was also a sort of jury, who didn't do much but just sit there and see fair play. Ten of them altogether—four women and six men; and you never saw them long, just a glimpse now and then, and it was specially hard to get a good look at the end man farthest away. Which was a pity so far as the others were concerned, because then they might have understood at once. But Mum, beginning to shake, didn't think this time it was somebody who looked like Uncle Phil, she knew very well it *was* Uncle

Phil. In fact, she couldn't be certain he hadn't given her one of his nasty looks.

"Una, just a minute," she said shakily, as soon as the newsreel started, and off she went into the back room, trusting that Una would have sense enough to follow her. The next minute they were staring at one another, out of sight and sound of the others, and Mum knew at once that Una was as worried as she was.

"You saw him at the end there, didn't you, Una?" she asked, after giving herself time to catch her breath.

"Yes, and this time I thought it really *was* him," said Una.

"I *know* it was. I'll take my dying oath it was."

"Oh—Mum—how could it be?"

"Don't ask me how it could be," cried Mum, nearly losing her temper. "How should I know? But there he was—yes, and I'm not sure he didn't give me one of his looks."

"Oh—dear!" Una whispered, her eyes nearly out of her head. "I was hoping you wouldn't say that, Mum. Because I thought he did too, then I thought I must have been making it up."

"Una, that's three times already," said Mum, not sharp now but almost ready to cry. "I'm certain of it now. That was him in the film. That was him in the boxing. Don't tell me it's a what's-it—just accidental. He's there."

"Where?"

"Now don't start acting stupid, Una. How do I know where? But already we've seen him three times, and if I know him this is only his first try. It'll be a lot worse soon, you'll see. It's just like him trying to spoil our pleasure."

"Oh—Mum—how could he? Listen, I believe we were thinking about him——"

"I wasn't thinking about him——"

"I expect you were and you didn't know it," Una continued with some determination. "Same with me. Then we think we see him——"

"I *know* I saw him," cried Mum, exasperated. "How many times have I to keep telling you?"

"You'll see—it'll wear off."

"Wear off! You'll get no wearing off from him. I tell you, he's there, just to spite us, and he's staying there. You watch!"

While they were staring at one another, not knowing what to say next, Steve popped his head in. "Come on, you two. Bathing show next. Boy—oh boy!" Then he vanished.

"You go, Una," said Mum, her voice trembling. "It'll look funny if neither of us goes, and I can't face him again tonight. I'm going to make myself a cup of tea. Honestly, I'd give the show away if I went."

"Well," said Una, hesitating, "I suppose I ought. I can't see how he could be there—and I believe it's all our fancy. But if I did see him again, I'd scream—couldn't stop myself." And she went off rather slowly to the front room.

Mum was just pouring out her tea when she heard the scream. The next moment Una came flying in, followed by her husband, who looked annoyed. "Mum, he was there again."

"What's the idea?" George demanded, like a policeman.

"I'll tell him," cried Mum. "You sit down and drink that tea, Una dear. Now then, George Fleming, you needn't look at me like that. Just listen for once. Una's upset because she must have seen Uncle Phil again. We'd seen him three times before—and that must have been the fourth. He was there again, wasn't he, Una? Yes, well I'm not surprised." She looked severely at George, daring him to laugh. "He was there, wasn't he? Tell me the truth now, George."

"Why should I lie?" said George, not even smiling. "I'll admit it's quite a coincidence. Twice I noticed a chap who looked very like Uncle Phil——"

"Four times I've seen him now," cried Una, sitting with her cup of tea. "Honestly I have, George."

"And you can't explain it, can you?" And now George *was* smiling, as he looked from one harassed woman to the other.

"How can anybody explain it?" said Mum crossly. "He's there, that's all."

"Come off it, Ma," said George. "You'll be telling me

next he's haunting us. Couldn't be done. Let's have a bit of common. I can explain it."

"Oh—George—can you?" Una was all relief, gratitude and devotion.

"Certainly." George waited a moment, enjoying himself. Mum could have slapped him. "Look—they have to have a lot of chaps round when they're doing these scenes—chaps with the cameras, lights and all that. Well, it just happens that one of 'em—who keeps getting into the picture when he oughtn't—looks like Uncle Phil—head on one side and so forth. And this set reminds you of Uncle Phil—bought with his money—so every time you see this chap you tell yourself it must be him, though of course it couldn't be—stands to reason."

"That's it, George," cried Una. "Must be. Mum—we were just being silly."

But Mum, who could be very obstinate at times, wasn't so easily persuaded. "I see what you mean, George. But I don't know. I can't believe these television chaps are as old as that. And what about that look he gave me?"

"Oh—come off it," said George, losing his patience. "You imagined that. How could the chap take a look at you? He was just looking at the camera, that's all. Now let's pack this up and go back and enjoy ourselves. Come on—some variety turns next. You don't want to spoil it for everybody, do you?"

This artful appeal was too strong even for Mum's misgivings, and George triumphantly escorted them to the front room. The variety show was about to begin; already a band was playing a lively tune. Mum found herself looking round with satisfaction at the expectant faces of her family. This was more like it, what she'd hoped for from a television set.

Three girls did a singing and dancing turn, to start off with, and it wasn't bad. Ernest, who was sitting next to Mum, breathed hard at them, but whether out of approval or disapproval, she didn't know. Since that dark fancy girl at the confectioner's had given him up, Ernest had seemed to be off women, but of course you could never tell, steady as he was. Next turn was a nice-looking young chap who played an accordion, and Mum felt secretly in agreement with Joyce who loudly declared he was 'smashing'. He finished off with some nice old panto songs that they all began to sing. Now at last Mum felt really happy with the set. And of course just after that was when it had to happen.

A conjurer appeared, a big comical fellow who pretended to be very nervous. George told them he was the top turn of the show, very popular. He did one silly trick and then pretended to do another and make a mess of it, which made them all laugh a lot. Then he said he'd have to have somebody from the audience, though there wasn't any audience to be seen. As soon as he said that, as Mum told them afterwards, she suddenly felt nervous. And then there he was, giving them a nasty sideways grin—Uncle Phil.

"I won't have it," Mum screamed, jumping up. "Turn it off, turn it off." But before anyone could stop her, she had turned it off herself. As they gaped at her, she stood in front of the set and stared at them defiantly.

"What's the matter with you?" cried Dad, looking at her as if she'd gone mad. And as the others all began talking, he turned on them: "Now you be quiet. I'm asking Mum a question. We can't all talk at once."

Joyce started giggling and Steve gave a loud guffaw, as boys of that silly age always do.

"Do you mean to say, Fred Grigson," said Mum, glaring at him, "that you haven't noticed him yet? Five times—counting the one I didn't see but Una did—he's turned up already, and this is only the first night we've had it. Five times!"

"What you talking about?" asked Dad angrily. "Five times what? Who's turned up?"

"Uncle Phil," said Una quickly, and then burst into tears. "I've seen him every time." And she went stumbling out of the room, with George, who was a good husband for all his faults, hurrying after her.

Dad was flabbergasted. "What's the matter with her? I wish you'd talk sense. What's this about Uncle Phil?"

"Oh—don't be such a silly donkey," cried Mum. "He keeps coming into these television pictures. Haven't you got any eyes?"

"Eyes? What's eyes got to do with it?" Dad shouted, thoroughly annoyed now. "I've got some sense, haven't I? Phil's dead and buried."

"I know he is," said Mum, nearly crying. "That's what makes it so awful. He's doing it on purpose, just to spoil it for us."

"Spoil it for us?" Dad thundered. "You'll have me out of my mind in a minute. Here, Ernest, did you see anybody that looked like Uncle Phil?"

Later, round the supper table, they sorted it out. Una and Mum were certain they had seen Uncle Phil himself five and four times respectively. George said he had seen a camera man, or somebody who looked like Uncle Phil, three times. After maddening deliberation, Ernest agreed with George. Joyce said she had twice seen somebody who looked the spit image of Uncle Phil. Steve kept changing his mind, sometimes agreeing with his mother and Una, sometimes joining the Coincidence School. Dad from first to last maintained that he had seen nobody that even reminded him of Uncle Phil and that everybody else had Uncle Phil on the brain.

"Now you just listen to me, Dad," said Mum finally. "I know what I saw and so does Una. And never mind about any coincidences. They wouldn't make me jump every time like that. Besides I know that look of his, couldn't miss it."

"How on earth——" Dad began, but she wouldn't let him go on.

"Never mind about *how on earth*," Mum shouted. "Because I don't know and you don't know and nobody does. What I'm telling you is that he's got into that set somehow and there'll be no getting him out. It'll get worse and worse, you mark my words. And if we've any sense we'll ask Alf Stocks to take that set away and give us our money back."

This roused George, who made himself heard above the

others. "Oh—come off it, Ma. Alf Stocks would never stop laughing if we told him he'd have to take that set back because Uncle Phil's haunting it. Now—be reasonable. You and Una got excited and started imagining things. Everything'll be okay tomorrow night, you'll see."

"Oh—will it? That's what you say."

"Of course it's what I say. It's what we all say."

"Have it your own way," said Mum darkly. "Just keep on with it. But don't say I didn't warn you. He's there—and he's staying there—and if you ask me, this is only the start of it. He'll get worse before he gets better. Wherever he is, he's made up his mind we shan't enjoy a television set bought with his insurance money. You'll see."

In the middle of the following afternoon, when Mum and Una had the place to themselves and usually enjoyed a quiet sensible time together, they were both restless. They had gone into the front room, to sit near the windows and keep an eye on the street below, but it was obvious that they would never settle down. There in its corner was the TV set with its screen that looked like an enormous blind eye. For some minutes they pretended not to notice it. Finally, Una said: "I looked in the *Radio Times* and there's a programme for women this afternoon."

"I know," said Mum rather grimly. "I looked too."

"We'd be all right with that, surely? In any case——"

"In any case—what?" Mum still sounded rather grim.

"Well," said Una timidly, "don't you think we might have got a bit worked up last night—and—imagined things?"

"No, I don't," said Mum. Then, after a moment: "Still, if you want to turn it on—turn it on. If it's a women's programme—middle of the afternoon too—perhaps he won't show up. He used always to have a sleep in the afternoon."

"But—listen, Mum. As George says——"

"Never mind what George says. George doesn't know it all even though you'd sometimes think he does. But go on—turn it on, if you want to."

Una walked across and rather gingerly manipulated the switches. With an absent-minded air, Mum arrived in front of the set and sat down in a chair facing it. The next minute they were looking at and listening to the matron of a girls' hostel, a woman so determinedly refined that she sounded quite foreign.

"You see, it's all right," said Una, when the matron had been followed by two girls playing the violin and piano.

"So far," said Mum, "but give him time. Still—this is very nice, I must say."

After the music a man came on to talk about buried treasure. He was a youngish chap, schoolmaster type, very nervous and sweating something terrible. "You'd be surprised at what some of us have found," he told them. "And now I want to show you a few things—genuine treasure trove." He beckoned anxiously to somebody off the screen, saying: "If you don't mind—thank you so much."

It was Uncle Phil who walked on, carrying some of the things, and as soon as he was plainly in view he turned that twisted neck of his, looked straight out at Mum and Una, and said: "Talk about treasure! You Grigsons haven't done so bad with that hundred-and-fifty quid of mine."

"You see—talking to us now," screamed Mum as she dashed forward. "But I'll turn him off." And as she did, she added firmly: "And that's the last time he does that to me. I'll not give him another chance. God knows what he'll be saying soon!" She pointed an accusing finger at Una, who was still trembling in her chair, and went on: "I suppose we're still a bit worked up and just imagined *that*. Now, Una—you saw him, you heard him—didn't you? Right, then. No going back on it this time."

And Mum marched out and made for the kitchen, where she clattered and banged until it was time for a cup of tea. Steve, who worked in an auctioneer's office and kept odd hours there, was the first home that day, and without saying a word to his mother and sister he hurried straight through into the front room, obviously making for the television set. The two women, who were in the back room, preparing the evening meal, said nothing to him. This, as Una guessed at once, was Mum's new line; no more protesting, no more trying to convince the others; just a grim dark silence, waiting for the final din and flare of 'I told you so'. As they laid the table, they could hear voices from the set but no actual words. Five minutes, ten minutes, passed.

Then abruptly the voices from the front room stopped. There was a silence that lasted perhaps half a minute, and then Steve, looking quite peculiar, came slowly into the back room. He tried to avoid meeting the questioning stares of the two women. He sat down and looked at the dining-table. "Nearly ready?" he enquired, in a small choked voice.

"No it isn't nearly ready," said Mum. "You're very early today. Why did you switch that set off like that?"

"Oh—well," said Steve, wriggling, "didn't seem much point in bothering with a dreary old flick."

This wretched performance hadn't a chance even with Una, and of course Mum could read him as if he were a theatre poster. "Stop that silly nonsense," said Mum. "You saw him, didn't you?"

"Saw who?"

"You know very well who—your Uncle Phil. Didn't you?"

"Well, yes, I thought I did," said Steve carefully.

"Thought you did! You saw him nearly as plain as you can see me, didn't you?"

"No—but I did see him." Steve was clearly embarrassed.

"Did he say anything—I mean, to you?"

"Now, Mum, how *could* he——"

"Stop that," shouted Mum. "I'm having no more of that nonsense. And just you tell your mother the honest truth, Steve. Now—did he say anything to *you*? And if so—what?"

The youth swayed from side to side and looked utterly miserable. "He said I took two shillings of his."

The women gasped. "Now isn't that just like him?"

cried Mum. "And you never took two shillings of his, did you?"

"Yes, I did," Steve bellowed unhappily, and then charged out, so that he seemed to be pounding down the stairs before they had time to raise any protest.

"Just what I thought," said Mum before going into her terrible grim silence again. "It'll get worse, like I said."

Sometimes it was nice when the men came up from the shop like boys out of school, hearty and boisterous; and then at other times it wasn't. This was one of the other times. And unfortunately they had decided that the idea of Uncle Phil appearing on television programmes was Humorous Topic Number One, and roared round the place making bad jokes about it. With her lips almost folded away, Mum heard them in the grimmest of silences. Una caught George's eye once or twice, but there was no stopping him. How much was the B.B.C. paying Uncle Phil? Had he got his Union card yet? Would they be starring him in a show soon? And couldn't Ma take a joke these days?

"We haven't all got the same sense of humour, George Fleming," she told him. "And now I'm going out. I promised to go and see Mrs. Pringle."

Una looked dubious. It was the first she had heard of any visit to Mrs. Pringle, and Mum liked to discuss her social engagements well in advance. "Shall I come too?" she asked nervously.

"No reason why you shouldn't, Una dear," Mum replied grandly. "We can leave these men to have a nice evening of television. And I hope they enjoy it." And off she went, with Una trailing behind.

A little later, when he had his pipe going, Dad said to George: "Well, that's how they are, and always will be, I expect. Moody. One day they're all for a television set, must have it. Next day, just because of some silly nonsense, won't look at it. Hello!"—this was to Joyce, who came hurrying in—"where've you been, girl?"

"Where d'you think?" cried Joyce. "Working. No, I don't want anything to eat. I'll have something in the Empire caffy. We're going there."

"What's the use of spending all this money on a television set," Dad shouted as she ran upstairs, "if you're going to waste more money at the Empire?"

She stopped long enough to shout down: "You've not talked to Steve, have you?"

"No, haven't seen him yet."

"Well, I have," she cried triumphantly. And that was the last of her.

Dad and George did not wait for Ernest, for they knew he would be late, this being his night for attending his Spanish class. (Nobody knew why he was learning Spanish; perhaps it helped to keep him steady.) So after clearing the table and doing a bit of slapdash washing up (just to show Mum), they moved luxuriously, in a cloud of tobacco smoke, into the front room. They were, as they knew, just in time for *Television Sports Magazine*, a sensible programme they could enjoy all the better for not having a pack of impatient bored women with them.

The first chap to be interviewed for this *Sports Magazine* was a racing cyclist, who could pedal like mad but was no great shakes at being interviewed, being a melancholy youth apparently suffering from adenoids. However, Dad and George had a good laugh at him, legs and all.

"And now for a chat with a typical old sportsman," said the Sporting Interviewer, all cast-iron geniality, "the sort of man who's been watching cricket and football matches and other sporting events for the last sixty years or so. Welcome to Television, Mr. Porritt!"

Mr. Porritt, who came strolling into the picture, was small, old, bent. He carried his head to one side. He had a long and rather frayed nose, and an evil little eye. And without any shadow of doubt he was Uncle Phil.

"No," cried Dad, "it can't be."

"Let's hear what he says," cried George. "Then we'll know for certain."

"Now, Mr. Porritt, you've been watching sport for a good long time, haven't you?" said the Interviewer.

"That's right," said Uncle Phil, grinning and giving Dad and George a wicked look. "Saw a lot o' sport, I did, right up to the time when I had the bad luck to go and live at Smallbridge, with a family by the name of Grigson. That finished me for sport—and for nearly everything else."

"How d'you mean?" shouted Dad, jumping up.

"Shop-keeping people," Uncle Phil continued, "in a petty little way—frightened o' spending a shilling or two——"

"No, don't turn him off," shouted George, almost going into a wrestling match with his father-in-law. "Let's hear what he has to say."

"If you think I'm going to sit here listening to slurs and insults," Dad bellowed. "Take your hands off me."

"Listen—listen—look—look!" And George succeeded in holding Dad and keeping him quiet for a few moments.

"Yes, indeed," Mr. Porritt was saying, in rather a haw-haw voice, "the first Test match I ever attended—dear me—this is going back a long time——"

"It's not him now," Dad gasped. "Quite different." Which was true, for the Mr. Porritt they saw and heard now was not at all like Uncle Phil. After a moment or two, Dad said quietly: "Now, never mind Test matches, George. Turn it off. We've got to have a talk about this."

Even though the screen was dark and silent, they both instinctively moved away from it and sat down by the fireplace. "Now then, George," Dad began, with great solemnity, "we've got to get this straight. Now did you or did you not think that Mr. Porritt, when he first started, was Uncle Phil?"

"I was almost certain he was," replied George, who had lost his usual self-confidence. "Last night, I'll admit, I thought it was some B.B.C. chap who happened to look a bit like him——"

"Never mind about last night," said Dad hurriedly. "And did you or did you not hear him talk about us—very nasty of course——?"

"I did," said George, who began to feel he was in a witness box.

"So did I," said Dad, and then, perhaps realising that this bald statement was something of an anti-climax, he raised his voice: "And it don't make sense. Couldn't happen. Here's a man who's dead and buried——"

"I know, Dad, I know," cried George hastily. "And I agree—it couldn't happen——"

"Yes, but it *is* happening——"

"Not really," said George, looking very profound.

"How d'you mean—*not really*?" cried Dad, nettled. "Saw and heard for yourself, didn't you?"

"If you ask me," said George slowly and weightily, "it's like this. Uncle Phil's not in there, couldn't possibly be. He's on our minds, in our heads, so we just *think* he's there. And of course," he continued, brisker now, "that's what was the matter with Una and Mum. They kept seeing him last night, like they said, and you can bet your boots they saw and heard him—or thought they did—today, before we came up from the shop. And I'll tell you another thing, Dad. Young Steve dashed out again, before we were back, didn't he? And Joyce said she'd talked to him."

"You think they got mixed up in it, do you?"

"Young Steve was, I'll bet you anything. And whatever it was he saw and heard, it sent him out sharp and upset Mum and Una—see?"

Dad re-lit his pipe but performed this familiar operation rather shakily. His voice had a tremble in it too. "This is a nice thing to happen to decent respectable people. Can't amuse themselves quietly with a TV set—hundred-and-twenty-pound set too—without seeing a kind of ghost—who starts insulting 'em. Here, George, do you think all the other people hear what he says?"

"No, of course they don't. They just hear Mr. Porritt."

"But it isn't Mr. Porritt all the time."

"I know—but I mean, whoever it ought to be. Don't you see," and George leant forward and tapped Dad on the knee, "we only imagine he's there."

This annoyed Dad. "But why should I imagine he's there? I'll tell you straight, George, I'd had more than enough of Brother Phil when he was alive, without any imagining. All I wanted tonight was a *Sports Magazine*—not any insults from that miserable old sinner. I call this downright blue misery."

They were still arguing about it, without taking another look at the set, when Ernest came in. "Hello," he said, "aren't we having any television tonight?"

"No," said Dad, and was about to explain why when George gave him a sharp nudge.

"Just having an argument about something we heard on it earlier," said George. "You turn it on whenever you like, Ernest."

Ernest said he would as soon as he had put on his slippers and old coat, which was something he always made a point of doing when he came home in the evening. And while Ernest was outside, George explained to Dad why he had given him that nudge. "Let's see what Ernest makes of it."

"I don't see Ernest imagining anything," said Dad. "If Ernest sees Uncle Phil, then Uncle Phil's there all right."

"Now then," said Ernest, a few minutes later, as he looked at the *Radio Times*, "—ah—yes—*Current Conference*—a discussion programme, I believe. That should be interesting—and we're just in time for it." He sounded like somebody, the ideal stooge, taking part in a dull programme.

When the set came to life, George and Dad rather stealthily moved nearer. Ernest had planked himself dead in front of it, looking as if TV had been invented specially for him. The screen showed them some chaps sitting round a table, looking pleased with themselves. The room was immediately filled with the sound of their voices, loud and blustering in argument. The camera moved around the table, and sometimes went in for a close-up. These politicians and editors seemed to be arguing about the present state of the British People, about which they all apparently knew a great deal. A shuffling at the door made Dad turn round, and then he saw that Mum and Una had returned and were risking another peep. They ignored him, so he pretended he hadn't seen them. Meanwhile, the experts on the British People were all hard at it.

"And now, Dr. Harris," cried the Chairman, "you've a good deal of specialised knowledge—and must have been thinking hard—so what have you to say?" A new face appeared on the screen, and it belonged to a head that was held on one side and had a long nose and the same old wicked look. Dr. Harris nothing! It was the best view of Uncle Phil they had had yet.

"What have I to say?" Uncle Phil snarled. "Zombies. Country's full o' zombies now. Can't call 'em anything else. Don't know whether they're alive or dead—and don't care. Zombies. And if you want an example, just take Ernest Grigson of Smallbridge——"

"Stop it," screamed Mum from the doorway. "He gets worse every time."

George had the set switched off in three and a half seconds, probably a record so far.

Ernest looked dazed. "I must have dropped off," he explained to them all, "because I seemed to see Uncle Phil and thought he mentioned my name——"

"And so he did, you pie-can," roared Dad. Then he turned to George: "I suppose you're going to say now we all imagined that together. Urrr!"

"It's just his wicked devilment," cried Mum, coming in and joining them now. "Is this his first go tonight?"

"Not likely, Ma," said George, and explained what had happened to the *Sports Magazine*.

"Personal slurs and insults every time now," said Dad bitterly.

"But wait a minute," said Ernest, looking more dazed

than ever and speaking very carefully. "Even if he was alive, they wouldn't have Uncle Phil on that *Current Conference* programme. I mean to say, they only have——"

"Oh—for goodness sake, Ernest!" cried Una. "What's the use of talking like that? I'll scream in a minute."

Mum looked severely at the men. "Now you'll perhaps believe me when I tell you what happened when Una and me turned it on earlier—yes, and what happened to poor Steve." And they had to listen to a very full account of Uncle Phil's earlier appearances, together with some references to his antics on the screen the previous night. This led to a further and still noisier argument between George and Dad, on meta-physical lines, turning on whether Uncle Phil was really there or was being projected into the screen by their imagination. Just when it was becoming unbearably complicated, it was sharply interrupted.

A little procession of young people marched into the room. Steve had a youth his own age with him, and Joyce, looking pale but determined, was accompanied by two watery-eyed spluttering girl friends and a scared-looking boy friend.

"Now what's the idea, you two?" cried Dad, annoyed at being silenced.

"We've been talking," said Joyce, who had a will of her own, "and now I'm going to turn that set on, just to see for myself, and nobody's going to stop me." She looked so fierce that nobody attempted to stop her. "What's supposed to be on now?"

"One of those pieces about crime not paying," George told her as she went across to the switches.

They all looked and listened in silence. A rather dolled-up woman appeared on the screen, and was saying: "Well, that's one point of view. And now for another. What do you think, Inspector Ferguson?"

"Here we go," muttered George. "I'll bet you a quid."

There was a gasp from all the Grigsons. This time Uncle Phil's horrible sharp face filled the whole screen, and his voice, when it came, was louder than they had ever heard it before. This time even Mum had to listen.

"Take the case of an elderly man with heart disease," said Uncle Phil, already with a gleam in his eye. "When an attack comes on, he has to crush some pill things in his mouth—or he's a goner. And suppose somebody—just a young niece perhaps—deliberately puts those life-savers out of his reach— so when he has an attack he'll finish himself trying to get to them—it's a kind of murder——"

"Not on purpose I didn't—you dirty lying old weasel!" Joyce screamed, and then threw the stool at the screen.

Next morning, Alf Stocks was there, shaking his head at Mum. "No use telling me it's brand-new and priced at a hundred-and-twenty. Tube's done in, see—that's the trouble. I'm taking a chance offering you twenty-five for it. Yes, I dare say it was an accident, but then some accidents——" and then, as Mum said afterwards, he gave her a sharp, sideways, old-fashioned look—"are very expensive."

GUEST OF HONOUR

Sir Bernard Clipter was on his way to a dinner of the Imperial Industrialists' Association. There were four of these dinners every year, and Sir Bernard had attended at least a score of them. But this was a special occasion, for tonight he was to be the chief guest of honour. There would be speeches in his praise; his health would be drunk; and his reply, which would give him an opportunity of discussing their joint problems, would probably be the principal speech of the evening. His notes for it, carefully typed in capital letters, were in his inside pocket waiting for the moment when he would be called upon to rise. Some of the biggest men in industry would be there tonight to honour him. Some politicians and important journalists too. So Sir Bernard really felt the proud man that he had already declared himself to be in the notes for his speech.

"Mr. Chairman, My Lords, Gentlemen," he heard himself beginning, but then he stopped this foolish rehearsing, which did a man no good at this last minute. He flicked a thin gold watch out of his dress waistcoat and examined its face in the uncertain light that reached him through the window of his Rolls. He was late. Sharply he signalled his chauffeur to hurry, although there was not much the man could do about it, for the traffic was still thick here in Piccadilly. A few moments later, just when the chauffeur was trying to pick up some speed, the little accident occurred.

Suddenly the formidable braking power of the car was applied, with the result that the car stopped, but Sir Bernard, who had no brakes of his own, shot forward and had to clutch the wide-open window for support. This brought him within sight of—and indeed quite close to—the fellow who had been the cause of the trouble. The chauffeur was turning round, shouting angrily at the fellow, who was a shabby-looking oldish man, possibly a foreigner; and now Sir Bernard, still clutching the window, had to relieve his feelings too.

"Why the devil don't you look where you're going, you idiot?" he roared, glaring and thrusting out his powerful jaw.

It was clear that the man had been startled by the Rolls, but now he showed no fear of Sir Bernard. He had curious eyes, of a pewter shade and with no whites visible round them; and for a second, as he stared at Sir Bernard, these eyes seemed enormous, like dark frozen lakes.

"Tonight," said the man, who spoke like a foreigner, "you look where you are going."

Then the Rolls went on its majestic way. Settling back again, Sir Bernard found that his earlier mood of pleased anticipation had been broken completely by this incident. Not that the man's eyes—though they really were very odd—troubled him. Or that bit of impertinence about his looking where he was going tonight—probably all that a bewildered foreigner could think of saying by way of a retort. To encounter the sudden wrath of Sir Bernard Clipter, as a great many employees of industry knew only too well, was no joke. No, Sir Bernard reflected sombrely, the trouble was—blood pressure, as the specialist had warned him. Something went wrong, he lost his temper like that, and then his heart went pounding away, leaving him feeling breathless and rather apprehensive as he did now. *Tonight, you look where you are going.* Well, the frightened half-wit had to say something. And Sir Bernard reminded himself that he might indeed have to look where he was going from tonight onwards. Some of the political and newspaper men, hearing what was said about him and what he would have to say himself, all with the approval of the powerful I.I.A., might soon be declaring that the nation could use and honour Sir Bernard Clipter even more than it had done up to now. Oh yes—from tonight he might have to look where he was going.

When he could see the main entrance of the Cosmopolis Hotel, where the dinner was being held, Sir Bernard took another look at his watch. Not too bad. He was late but not disgracefully so. Probably he would just have time to swallow one cocktail before the Chairman, old Lord Cooping, made for the dining-room. An absurd thing happened then, just as Sir Bernard pushed himself out of his seat. The giant doorman of the Cosmopolis, whom he had often seen, hurried forward to open the door, and by some odd trick of light turned for a fraction of a second into a skeleton.

"Thought you were a skeleton for a moment," said Sir Bernard, laughing, as he stepped out. The doorman of course looked the same as usual.

"Well, I suppose I am, sir," said the doorman.

Sir Bernard frowned and paid no further attention to the man. No need for the fellow to be so pert. Some of these fellows, who probably made two or three thousand a year out of tips and paid no income tax, were getting spoilt. Well, that would be the last friendly humorous remark any of his type would hear from Sir Bernard for the next day or two.

He had to go through the main lounge of the hotel and then along a corridor to find the large private dining-room where the I.I.A. function was being held. Nothing strange happened of course—why should it?—and all that Sir Bernard noticed was that the lighting of the Cosmopolis seemed to be rather poor. Either that or his eyes were giving some trouble again. It was not so much that the place itself seemed underlit. But the people were so dim. If he had had to meet some people either in the lounge or the corridor, he felt he would never have been able to recognise them. Odd effect—just seeing vague shapes in chairs!

But here was the red-coated Toastmaster, the usual fellow, who recognised him. And here was old Cooping, looking like a decayed pink bloodhound. As he drank his cocktail and listened to Lord Cooping's remarks about the guests and speakers, Sir Bernard experienced a feeling of relief that everything here seemed so normal, and then immediately afterwards felt annoyed with himself for needing to be reassured. Why shouldn't everything be normal? What was the matter with him? Nerves—because he had to make an important speech? Or that little shaking up in the car?

Now they were going into the dining-room, which looked very imposing, and old Cooping was still talking. "Never occurred to me before, Clipter," he was saying, "but here you are—member of the Association, been one for years of course—yet tonight we call you Guest of Honour. Very irregular really—though I don't suppose it matters. Can't be a guest, though, if you're a member. Secretary ought to have remembered that. We're sitting over there, I think."

As Sir Bernard followed the large shambling figure of Lord Cooping, another strange thing happened, all in a flash. Suddenly he knew that the old man was near death and was now so desperately weary that he longed for it. And this function meant nothing to him but so much added weariness. He had not been able to refuse when they had begged him to take the Chair, but there was nothing left in him that responded to the occasion. It was to him so much dreary mockery, merely part of a sick dream. He would thank God when the last self-important ass had said his say and they could all go home. And all this Sir Bernard realised as sharply as if he had been feeling it himself. Yet Lord Cooping was no friend of his; they really didn't much like each other. Nor was Sir Bernard in the habit of sharing other people's feelings. Since his wife's death and his quarrel with his daughter, soon after her idiotic marriage, he had never felt close to anybody, and indeed had found it easier to get on with his work and to enlarge his public life now that he was free of any entanglement with other people's feelings. Yet here he was, with an important occasion on his hands, suddenly being invaded by old Cooping's misery. He decided, in his own phrase, to pull himself together.

Pulled together, he was able to look round at the tables with some pleasure and pride. There must have been about two hundred men there (no women at these dinners), and they represented a very solid and impressive pyramid of achievement and power. He gave a wave to several men he knew well, and smiled at various business acquaintances, there to do him honour. He glanced at the Toast list. Sir Geoffrey Rawlands, a very solid man about his own age, was down to propose his health. Pember, of United Metals, youngish and only recently come to the top, was to second Rawlands; and Sir Bernard could not help feeling pleased that one of the most brilliant of the younger men had consented to say something pleasant about him in public. And Brexley, now in the Cabinet, was to reply for the general guests. The Association was doing him proud. This was indeed an occasion; and the central figure of it might well have to look where he was going. Silly to remember that, though.

At last the waiters began serving the soup. From his place in the middle of the speakers' table, Sir Bernard had a good view of them. At ordinary times he would not have thought them worth a second glance. But this was not an ordinary time. He could not help staring at these waiters, who looked quite different from the usual run of waiters and quite unfit to be serving an important dinner at the Cosmopolis Hotel. They still appeared to move quickly but they seemed to be doing it in their sleep. As if fifty somnambulists had taken to serving soup. The effect was horrible. Nor was that all, for somewhere behind this sleep-walking, it seemed to Sir Bernard, there was a suggestion, deeply disturbing, of ill-will, of instinctive malignity. They might have been figures in some ballet or spectacle, so many robot poisoners.

Sir Bernard took another pull at himself. He prided himself on not being a fanciful man; he lived—and had succeeded—in a world where facts were all-important; and this was certainly not the time to start being fanciful. At that moment, Parisi, the banquet manager of the Cosmopolis, arrived behind them to ask Lord Cooping if all was well. Sir Bernard had known Parisi ever since that plump smiling Italian had been assistant manager of the Grill, and now he turned to give him a sharp challenging look.

"Everatheeng all right, Sir Bernard?" asked Parisi.

"Not sure. What's the matter with these waiters of yours?" And as he asked this question, Sir Bernard suddenly realised that it was stupid, that there couldn't be anything wrong with the waiters, that he himself was somehow to blame.

Parisi's broad face registered extreme astonishment. "The waiters? My usual crew. Gooda men—much experience. You have some complaint, Sir Bernard?"

His tone was deferential. There was nothing different in his manner. But as Sir Bernard still stared up into the man's eyes, he seemed to see in them, somewhere in their depths, like a distant flame, something that was between contempt and anger and undoubtedly directed against himself. The smiling Parisi, whom he had known and patronised for so many years, hated him.

"No, no, Parisi, no definite complaint," he blustered. "But they look a queer bunch tonight. Look quite unlike the usual lot. Not the right types for this sort of affair."

It was ridiculous of course but it did seem to him then, just for one daft second, that not only was Parisi looking at him with contempt or anger or both, but that behind Parisi was a whole Italian family—a plump dark woman and several youths and girls—all giving him the same look. He turned away sharply, although Parisi was still murmuring some vague apology.

He told himself now that he had better keep quiet, no matter what he saw and heard—or thought he saw and heard. There was nothing wrong with this dinner. These sudden nightmare effects were his own doing. And then he remembered again: *Tonight, you look where you are going.* Not that it made any sense, for suddenly to see waiters as malignant sleep-walkers or to imagine a whole Parisi family hating him was not to look where he was going. All that had happened was that his mind had been astonishingly disturbed by this unimportant little incident. What he had to do, therefore, was to remember this, keep a tight hold on himself, and behave as if everything were normal, which indeed it was, outside the antics of his own mind.

"Sorry! What were you saying?" he asked Rawlands. He was seated between Lord Cooping, who was talking to Brexley, the Cabinet Minister, and the proposer of his toast, Sir Geoffrey Rawlands.

"I was saying that we ought to press for better co-ordination between the Ministry of Supply and the Board of Trade." Rawlands spoke with the cold deliberation of a man who dislikes having to repeat his words.

"Oh—yes—quite so," said Sir Bernard hastily. "You'll remember I brought that up at the last Association meeting. I thought I'd mention it again tonight—in my speech."

"So did I. And I'll be on first. But it'll do no harm if you mention it too, Clipter. I see we have the Press with us." Rawlands indicated the Press table over on their right.

But Sir Bernard did not look at the reporters. He was still staring at Rawlands, to whom he had turned when he had realised that he was not paying him sufficient attention. Rawlands was the burly type, red and solid as a side of beef. But as Sir Bernard stared at him, all that heavy beefiness seemed to thin out and melt away, although a shadowy outline remained, and what was left, still opaque and alive, was a meagre figure that used nothing of the familiar Sir Geoffrey Rawlands but his eyes. And there was a moment when it appeared as if this meagre anxious figure was clutching the hand of some woman, who was herself only a fleeting shadow. Sir Bernard summoned all his power of will, on which he not unreasonably prided himself, to dismiss these apparitions, to call back into plain sight the familiar ruddy bulk of Rawlands. And he succeeded.

"You all right, Clipter?" asked Rawlands, frowning.

"Yes, thanks. But tired. Overworking, as usual. Then—this speechmaking. You do more of it than I do, I think, Rawlands."

"I do too much of it. Keep myself too busy. Running from one thing to another. Don't give myself enough time to sit and think," said Rawlands.

"Because you're afraid, Geoffrey." It was a woman's voice, low-pitched, gentle. "You've always been afraid."

"What?" cried Sir Bernard.

"I say I don't give myself enough time to sit and think," said Rawlands, annoyed. "And neither do you, Clipter." Then he turned away.

Breathing hard, Sir Bernard tried to concentrate on the dinner he was eating. The sleep-walkers had now removed the soup plates and had already supplied the Chairman's table with portions of chicken and vegetables. For a minute or so, Sir Bernard ate and drank like a man who had just been lifted out of an open boat after a wreck. He noticed that neither the food nor the wine had any flavour. He might have been eating and drinking in a dream. This was no good, he decided. Why risk looking unmannerly, gobbling and swigging, when he couldn't even enjoy the stuff? He turned towards Lord Cooping, who was still talking to Brexley.

Again he felt strongly what Cooping was feeling—-the exhaustion, the weariness and boredom, the sense of being close to death. But now the feeling was stronger, less of a surprise and more of an ordeal for Sir Bernard. It compelled him to remember what he preferred always to forget, that we are all hurrying towards the grave, that nothing is certain for any of us except this final fact of death. And he did not, as he felt Cooping did, welcome this fact. It terrified him. What was the use of toiling to build up great enterprises, of planning to make himself and his fortunes so strong, so secure, when at any moment he might be tossed into the darkness, shovelled underground, no better off than the shabbiest clerk in his employment?

Hoping to rid himself of these unpleasant thoughts, he leaned forward so that he could observe and listen to Brexley, who was talking earnestly to Lord Cooping. Brexley was a wealthy man about fifty who had left industry for politics, and now he was frequently mentioned as a possible future Prime Minister. A sound man. Nothing weak and morbid about him. He wouldn't be waiting for death, like poor old Cooping. He was a rising man, in the prime of life, and looked it. So Sir Bernard bent forward, as far as dignity and comfort would allow, to look at and listen to Brexley. At this moment he felt he needed the company of a man who had, as people liked to say, a head on his shoulders.

Brexley still had a head on his shoulders but, as Sir Bernard saw with horror, it was now a very strange kind of head. For it looked like the head of a life-size talking doll. It was a doll that resembled Brexley, the coming man, the possible Prime Minister; it was wearing his clothes; it was complete with gestures and was able to swallow food and drink; but incontestably it was not a genuine human being at all—just a giant animated doll.

"He didn't make a good impression on the House," the doll was saying, nodding its head and rolling its eyes. "But of course that type of fellow rarely does. Lacks humanity, that's his trouble."

As Sir Bernard struggled with the nightmare effect, trying to change the doll back again into Brexley, chiefly by staring hard and telling himself that he knew very well Brexley was there all the time, a wine waiter arrived to fill his glass. The man's eyes were open but nevertheless he gave the impression of being fast asleep. His features were contorted into an appearance of appalling malignity. And he was saying something, although his lips did not appear to move. Sir Bernard listened carefully. "Night after night after night," the waiter was saying, "waiting on these self-satisfied swine—giving 'em wine they don't know how to appreciate—wasting the wine, wasting the nights, wasting my life——"

"Do you know what you're saying?" demanded Sir Bernard sharply.

"Oh—go and chase yourself," said the waiter.

"*What?*" Sir Bernard shouted. "What's that?"

"Beg your pardon, sir," said the waiter, in quite a different voice. "Did you say something?"

Sir Bernard felt that everybody near, perhaps everybody in the room, was staring at him. Had he shouted, and had everybody heard him? Fortunately—or so it seemed to him at that moment—the usual photographer who is present on these occasions now asked everybody to look at the camera and keep still for a moment or two. His camera looked gigantic, the largest Sir Bernard had ever seen.

"Now steady, please," cried the photographer. "By the way, it'll be an X-ray photograph, chiefly for the benefit of Sir Bernard Clipter."

Sir Bernard just managed to prevent himself from roaring out a question, asking the fellow what the blazes he meant by that outrageous remark. He had reached the conclusion that he could no longer trust what he thought he saw and heard. He seemed to be half in this dining-room and half in a nightmare. Soon the nightmare might take over altogether.

"Look at the death's head, everybody," cried the photographer. "This should be a very fine X-ray photograph, and I believe the Royal College of Surgeons will want at least one copy of it. Sir Bernard Clipter—please—try to keep that spinal column fairly straight. Now for the flash!"

It was nothing like the ordinary photographer's flashlight. There was far more of it, so that it hurt the eyes, blinding them with a lilac glare. When the smoke of it slowly cleared, the whole room seemed different. It seemed larger but dimmer. The clean black-and-white of the diners' clothes, the pink or purple of their faces, the varied tints, the glowing hues, of the flowers and wine and decorations, all appeared to have been dirtily bleached or covered with a film of grey; and the lights that glittered and sparkled before were now burning sullenly, so that the very atmosphere seemed thick and heavy. This was not a room in which any man could enjoy himself. It was a place in a terrifying bad dream.

"Mr. Chairman, My Lords, Gentlemen," cried the Toast-master, "pray see that your glasses are charged and pray silence for your Chairman." The words were the familiar words, but the voice was thin and high and might have had a wind whistling through it. Out of the corner of his left eye, Sir Bernard caught a glimpse of the face above the Toastmaster's red coat, and it was a face that was mostly whitened bone.

Lord Cooping proposed the Loyal Toast. Sir Bernard could hear him but he felt it was the tiniest voice he had ever been able to hear, a faint cry from the middle of some desert of exhaustion and utter weariness.

The cigar that Sir Bernard received with his coffee and brandy was an exceptionally fine-looking big Havana, and he lit it with unusual satisfaction. He felt there was something sane and comforting about a cigar. But not, he soon discovered, about this one. Its taste and smell were merely that of something burning—with less fragrance than a gardener's bonfire of weeds. And it turned to ash, a rather oily grey ash, spilling everything, at a shocking speed. Convinced that he had tried a faulty specimen, he took another, but that behaved in exactly the same fashion, offering no flavour, no fragrance, nothing but ash—ash—ashes.

"These cigars are terrible," he ventured to remark to Lord Cooping.

His lordship smiled, nodded. "Put yourself down for cremation, Clipter? Better do it in time. Lots of fellows who'd prefer cremation forget to give instructions. Insisted on it long ago myself." He leaned forward to address Sir Geoffrey Rawlands. "Ready when you are, Rawlands. All right?"

Sir Bernard, who had turned that way, saw an answering nod come from the shadowy bulk that was the outward Rawlands. He also saw, much clearer than before, the meagre figure inside, which now appeared smaller still but faintly luminous. It was the figure of a half-starved frightened child, and Sir Bernard could see that it was trembling and looking about wildly, as if for help in its distress. Was there the sound of a reedy voice, crying out of a child's panic fear? And did he hear again that low-pitched gentle woman's voice, responding, bringing consolation, offering courage.

Rawlands began his speech. Sir Bernard could hear the words, although the voice that pronounced them seemed small and distant; and he knew what the words meant, so that he realised that it was a good speech of its kind and that he himself was being praised in it. But all this was small and distant too. The speech had no more real significance than gabble overheard in a dream. It belonged to the world in which Rawlands was bulky, beefy and confident, a world of impudently deceitful appearances. In that world the meagre frightened child, still luminous in the shadowy cage of Rawlands's body, did not exist. And Sir Bernard could see that inner and more vital figure only too well. Impossible to ignore it.

At one point Brexley broke in with a loud complacent "Hear, hear!" and Sir Bernard took a quick look at him. What he saw was a six-foot doll in evening dress smoking a cigar. There were several similar dolls, nodding and smiling, further along the table.

The room seemed still larger and dimmer than ever. There were no longer any walls, only a fading into a grey mist. Some tables were occupied by nothing but skeletons, bobbing and swaying and sometimes bringing their bony hands together. Other tables had assorted animals, not like real animals but more like sinister toys. One or two of the tables at the back, or at least nearer the misty edge, were filled with nightmare creatures, out of the imagination of a child screaming in a dark room, creatures that were all huge eyes, beaks and snouts, claws and writhing tentacles. Another group, only just visible, had monster heads with idiot faces, smoking yard-long cigars and covering the table with grey ash.

There was the sound of applause; Rawlands had finished his speech. Then for one tantalising moment Sir Bernard had a glimpse of the large private dining-room of the Cosmopolis Hotel and two hundred members and guests of the Imperial

Industrialists' Association applauding a good after-dinner speech. The sensible scene remained to some degree, though it was hardly more than the coloured surface of a bubble, even when Lord Cooping was announcing that before the next speech some entertainers would perform an act. But then the bubble of sense burst, and lunacy and hell returned.

The entertainers were two men dressed in black from head to foot, with faces that might have been moulded out of white paper, and eyes that might have been holes burnt out of that paper. They carried a coffin made of some highly polished yellow wood. They arrived in silence but when they reached the centre of the room, which was dark now so that they could be sharply picked out by spotlights, they began chattering in high tones like idiots. This chatter was received with roars of laughter, but Sir Bernard found he could not understand a word of it. All he could gather, from their gestures, was that they were discussing the coffin. Finally, when they had reached screaming pitch, one of them thrust the other into the coffin. After a struggle, during which an arm or leg would come out and be savagely jammed in again, the victorious lunatic clapped on the lid, sat on it, and began to screw it down. Gales of laughter saluted this triumph. Then, to a final crescendo of applause, the victor, his mouth a wide red grin, dragged off the coffin, and the act was over.

Pember rose to speak. Unlike Rawlands, he looked his normal self, a rather tall, thin fellow of about forty, with untidy hair and brilliant eyes. Sir Bernard could not help regarding him with envy. He was the finest example of the new type of industrialist, a man who had not slugged his way to the top, making enemies all the way, but had arrived there, almost magically, from Cambridge laboratories and lecture rooms. Only forty—yet almost in command now of the empire of United Metals. He began to speak. At first Sir Bernard did not feel as he had when Rawlands was speaking that this speech had no real significance. It made good sense; there was genuine feeling in it too. The tribute he paid to Sir

Bernard, the latter felt, was a real tribute. For the first time since the dinner began, Sir Bernard's heart was warmed and comforted. He could make a friend of this brilliant younger man. No longer did he envy him; he liked him.

It was then that Sir Bernard saw the crab. It was no ordinary crab but a greenish-white creature that looked almost phosphorescent. When it first crawled up Pember's leg it was quite small, but then when it settled on his body and seemed to eat its way in, it grew and grew. It was feeding on Pember; and as its scaly carcase swelled out, Pember, still speaking, visibly lost weight and health until it was clear he was a dying man. And Sir Bernard, sick with fear, knew that this crab was cancer, and that Pember was indeed a doomed man. Then his compassion was so great that he closed his eyes, closed his mind as far as he could, to the whole dreadful scene; and the applause that came at the end of Pember's speech, the toast to himself (the moment he had been tasting in advance all the week), and some announcement by Cooping, seemed nothing more than faint noises from the street.

When he opened his eyes again he saw a midget woman prancing and gibbering in the spot-lighted space in the centre of the room, where the two lunatics with the coffin had performed. He did not want to look at this obscene little creature but found it impossible to ignore her. Followed by the spotlights she came nearer; and he realised with disgust that she was directing the words she screeched and her gestures at him, the guest of honour. She came nearer still, closer and closer, and then he knew why from the first he had thought her hateful and horrible, for she was like a parody of a girl he had known and loved years and years ago. It was as if this girl in all her foolish innocence had been pressed into a debased mould, injected with malignant obscenity, and then released to torment him. Nearer and nearer she came, waving her baby arms, pointing a tiny fat finger at him, wriggling her stunted body, contorting her over-size features that glistened with paint, until he felt that in another minute she would be crawling across the table to slobber in his arms. Crying out his disgust, he jerked back his chair. . . .

"Mr. Chairman, My Lords, Gentlemen," cried the Toastmaster. "Pray silence for your Guest of Honour—Sir Bernard Clipter."

As he rose, fumbling for the notes of his speech, there was much clapping and even some cheering. He saw that all the nightmare effects had vanished; he was in the Cosmopolis at a dinner of the I.I.A. Waiting for silence he had time to glance at Rawlands and then at Pember, and caught no glimpse of any meagre child or gnawing crab. There were no skeletons or monsters sitting at the tables; only solid middle-aged men waiting to hear him speak.

"Mr. Chairman, Sir Geoffrey Rawlands, Mr. Pember, My Lords and Gentlemen," he began. "I thank you most warmly for the way in which you have proposed this Toast and the way in which you have received it."

He paused for a moment there, as most speakers did when responding to such a toast, and then he saw among the faces turned to him at the nearest table one face that did not seem to belong to that or any other table of the I.I.A. It was the face of an oldish man, probably a foreigner; it was wide, flat and sallow, with large pewter-coloured eyes that seemed to have no whites round them. Yes, it was the face of the man who had said: "Tonight, you look where you are going." And from somewhere behind that face, out of those eyes, had come all the horrors of the evening. The sorcerer had arrived in person to discover how his spells were working.

With an immense effort Sir Bernard looked away from those extraordinary eyes. He glanced down at his notes. There was some impatient coughing. He fixed his gaze on the back of the room, though still aware of those eyes, and began: "The handsome compliments that have come my way tonight, gentlemen, I regard as tributes to our Association, and indeed to the industry of our British Commonwealth." This brought him a round of applause, and a breathing space. But then he saw a door open at the back. The two men in black entered, carrying the coffin. He forced himself to look somewhere else but this only brought him within the magnetic range of those eyes. He was sweating now. He put an arm up to his face, as if the lights were too bright for him, and said: "We are all industrialists here—except of course some of our distinguished guests." He removed the arm to indicate Brexley and turned himself in that direction. Brexley was a doll again, but a run-down doll now, badly in need of a good winding up. His head looked as if it might fall off.

"Two of our speakers," cried Sir Bernard desperately, "men of wide experience and exceptional knowledge, have already—er—touched on many of our present problems." The two men in black were now carrying the coffin shoulder-high, and perched on it, waving at him, was the midget woman. Behind them the wall had vanished again and the grey mist was there. Somewhere on the right, he knew, the tables of snouts, claws and tentacles and big-headed monsters were back again.

"But I should like to say something," he shouted, closing his eyes, "about the future of industry—especially the industry—the industry—the industrial development—of this country." He broke off, in despair, then opened his eyes and turned to old Lord Cooping. "Mr. Chairman—I must protest——"

"My dear Clipter," the old man murmured, out of a face as grey as the cigar ash that was everywhere, "please don't bother to protest—not to me. I'm dying—at last. Yes, it's here. . . ."

"Hear-hear-hear-hear-hear," muttered the Brexley doll, its hands flapping a little.

"But let us first of all take a glance at world markets," cried Sir Bernard.

The two men with the coffin and the midget woman were now only a few yards away. Behind them, climbing over the tables and pressing forward in solid ranks, were all the creatures and things he had seen earlier—the skeletons, the assorted toylike animals, the things with huge eyes, beaks, snouts, claws and tentacles, the big-heads with idiot faces.

"Yes—world markets," he screamed, making a final effort, "world markets—world markets—world markets——"

But it was no use. They were all coming nearer and nearer, and in another minute the obscene midget would be slobbering over him before the two men in black put him into the coffin and screwed the lid down over him while he heard the creatures and things yelling and screaming with maniac laughter. But even closer now was the man with the extraordinary eyes. He looked into them, crying for help, for mercy. . . .

He was looking out of the open window of his car, having shot forward when the chauffeur had to brake so suddenly. The cause of the trouble, a shabby-looking oldish man, possibly a foreigner, was standing there, staring in a daze out of curiously dull large eyes.

"Why the devil," he began explosively; but then checked himself. "You all right?"

A mild and friendly light came into those curious eyes, illuminating the broad sallow face. "Yes, thank you. I am sorry. I was dreaming."

"No harm done," said Sir Bernard, feeling an odd sense of relief. He settled back in his seat as the car moved away, and began to think about his speech, an important speech that he would shortly have to make as guest of honour at the dinner of the I.I.A.

LOOK AFTER THE STRANGE GIRL

THERE WAS a glassed-in passage that ran from the far end of the smoke-room to the big conservatory; it was probably a favourite sitting-out place at dances, and the basket chairs might have been left over there from some recent dance. Mark chose a chair, sagging and rather lop-sided, that was nearer the smoke-room than it was to the conservatory, so that he could still see the group round the piano. He could hear behind the singing and the piano the steady *chug-chug-chug*, from somewhere not far away, of the primitive electric light plant that Lord Broxwood had been boasting about at dinner. The voltage must be low and the bulbs could not be more than fifteen watt; they did not give much light but had a golden glow that was rather attractive. In the smoke-room, however, not far from the piano, there were also two large oil lamps. It was this lighting, low-toned, mellow and a trifle theatrical, Mark concluded, that brought the only suggestion of unreality to the scene.

He was smoking a very fat Egyptian cigarette and not enjoying it, but then there had been no sign of any Virginian cigarettes anywhere and he had not felt like tackling any of the cigars he had been offered after dinner. He was still feeling some bodily discomfort. It was some years since he had last worn white tie and tails, and of course these evening clothes were not his; and the collar was appallingly high. No wonder some of the older men looked apoplectic.

All the younger men and the girls were clustered round the piano, played with energy and not without skill by the monocled Captain Waterhouse; and now they were beginning in chorus 'Tell Me, Pretty Maiden' from *Florodora*, which Mark had heard on an old gramophone record. "Now tell me,

Pretty Maiden," roared the men, beefy and bold in their black-and-white, "are there any more at home like you?" And the girls, giggling a little and sounding very innocent with their wavering soprano, replied: "There are a few, Kind Sir, and better girls you never knew." With their hair piled so high, with such generous offerings of pink arms, white shoulders, plump soft bosoms, these girls seemed both larger and sillier than any girls he had known before. They aroused in him a vaguely lustful and predatory feeling, as if he were a schoolboy again and they were so many giant chocolate cakes. They made him understand all those winking references to 'girls' and 'curly-curls' in the old music-hall songs. He was now looking at the prettiest of all earth's extinct creatures. "Then take a little walk with me, and then we shall see," sang the men, having some difficulty with the rather subtle modulations of the tune, but loud and rich with masculine libido. They made him feel desiccated, about a thousand years old.

He dug the heels of his dress pumps, which did not fit him too well, deep into the coconut matting. First, just after it had happened, he had merely felt bewildered. Then for the next two or three hours, before and during dinner, he had felt frightened—of the fantastic situation he was in, and of any social complications it might produce, ending inevitably with questions that would have been an appalling embarrassment. (Thank God he had landed among this casual upper class, still so certain of themselves!) But now—and it was this and not fear that had driven him out of the smoke-room—he was possessed by a sense of loneliness that reached out and darkened to a feeling of utter desolation. The professional social historian in him was completely defeated; and even if he had had a notebook he could not have made a single note. All that the indomitable observer who never quite fails us could remark was that distance in time was apparently harder to bear than distance in space. Here he was, not two hundred feet away from his study and bedroom, but back in his own time he would have felt less desolate, he was certain, if he had suddenly found himself wandering on South Cape, Tasmania, half the globe away from home. Was home, then, more in time than in space? Yesterday he would have said No, he told himself, but now he was not sure. Odd how the young high spirits of the group round the piano, the sight of their flushed faces, the laughter breaking through the straggling chorus, widened and deepened his desolation.

But here was company; further need for care. For the elderly lady, plump and mottled, who had sat opposite to him at dinner came waddling in from the smoke-room, and sank with relief into the chair next to his. "I don't think we were introduced," she began. "They're always so casual here, especially when the youngsters have filled up the house. I'm Mrs. Buller—Lord Broxwood's sister—and, let me see, you're Ronald's friend, aren't you?"

This was rather tricky. "Well—yes—in a way."

"I'm abominably curious—my family are always teasing me about it—so don't mind. But wasn't there something about a bathing accident—Mr.-er-?"

"Denbow—Mark Denbow." What would she think, how would she behave, if he told her he had finished taking his evening seminar—yes, here in this house—at seven o'clock, had then hurried across to the lake for a quick dip before supper, and had dived—into all this? He gave her what he hoped was a friendly but apologetic smile. "Yes, I was bathing in the lake, and somehow lost consciousness—probably hit something when I dived in. And then your nephew—Ronald—fished me out."

"How fortunate!" Although she was so plump and smiling and comfortable, her eyes, with no more colour in them than a February sea, were cold. "One of his Oxford friends, I imagine, Mr. Denbow."

"I was at Oxford," said Mark, "but not with Ronald. As a matter of fact, we hadn't met before." One glance at her told him he could not leave it there. "I happened to be staying in this neighbourhood and—er—thought I'd bathe in the lake.

And after I'd got into difficulties and Ronald pulled me out," he continued, gaining confidence, "I was rather exhausted and he very kindly insisted on my spending the night here."

"That's so like Ronald," she said, smiling. "So brilliant too—even when he was a little boy he was quite shockingly clever. We all feel he has a great future."

And now what would happen if he gave Mrs. Buller a hard look, tapped her on her broad silken knee, and told her Ronald's future? For the memorial tablet in the chapel declared that Ronald had been (or would be) killed at Neuve Chapelle in 1915. But while he was making some vague agreeing noise by way of reply, Mrs. Buller found another topic.

"It's rather odd," she began, "but my niece Muriel followed her brother's example—so that there are two of you——"

"Two of us?" This really startled him.

"Oh—I don't mean this girl was bathing too. You probably haven't seen her because she didn't come down to dinner, not having anything decent to wear—mislaid her luggage apparently. Ann—something, I didn't catch her name. Indeed, I only caught a quick glimpse of the girl herself—a curious little creature. I gathered she'd been abroad—France, I believe—and arrived here, thinking it was some other house. And she'd walked from the station and been out in that dreadful thunderstorm, so Muriel, who's always sweet and kind, wouldn't let her go——"

"Was there a thunderstorm?" asked Mark innocently.

Mrs. Buller stared at him. "Where can you have been? The one that started just before six o'clock——"

"Oh—yes, of course," he cried. "How stupid of me! I ought to have remembered." But what he ought to have remembered was that Mrs. Buller's weather, before seven-fifteen tonight, was not his weather, belonging to a very different set of depressions and anti-cyclones.

"Ah—here's Dorothy—my daughter," cried Mrs. Buller, with maternal satisfaction. "Well, darling—are you tired of making a noise in there?"

Dorothy was a rather large, pretty girl in pink, all curves and down and delicate perspiration. She perched on the creaking arm of her mother's chair. "It's so jolly hot in there, Mummie," she said, smiling vaguely at Mark above her mother's head. "And I'm hoarse trying to sing. I hope they'll stop soon—and dance or something."

During the next few minutes, while the three of them talked and said nothing, Mark kept looking at Dorothy's eyes. They were bluer and altogether finer than her mother's, but what fascinated Mark was that they had a peculiar slanting set to them, and he remembered having noticed similar eyes in some elderly woman, quite recently. Nothing changes less about us, he knew, than the setting, the characteristic shape, of our eyes. And now he remembered whose eyes were set like these—they belonged to a member of the family here—old Lady Purzley. Were pink, smiling Dorothy and that grim old survivor, Lady Purzley, who had questioned him so ruthlessly about the school, the same person? He decided, as the hair on his neck felt queer, that they were.

Mrs. Buller thought she would try the card room, and gave Dorothy permission to show Mark the conservatory. It was almost big enough for Kew, and full of that rich tropical smell which arises from so much growth and yet seems to have more death in it than life. He had never seen it before; it must have been taken down or allowed to fall into decay just before or during World War Two. Among that cascading greenery, and the smell of warm damp earth, and in the dim undersea light of the place, Dorothy looked like some giant pink blossom that had set itself adrift. Yet somewhere along time's Scenic Railway, just before it dipped into the darkness, she would be Lady Purzley, gnarled in tweed, staring at him mistrustfully, opening thin and bitter lips to put insulting questions to him, before taking a not too unfriendly farewell of him and all the works of his kind. What was it she had said? "I suppose there's some point in all this adult education we're compelled to pay for, although the results are not very obvious. But I remember this house when it was full of young and hopeful life—brave young men who had manners, pretty girls who had charm——" And hearing Dorothy chattering on, he could now discover the likeness in the two voices. In his desolation he felt the need of some physical contact in this other time into which he had been thrust; so he put a hand under Dorothy's rounded elbow, presumably to guide her, then let it slide along her forearm until their hands met and, perhaps because she intuitively perceived his mood and need, their fingers interwined, and he felt her moist warm palm against his. He laughed, although he had no idea why he should.

"Why are you laughing?" she asked.

"I really couldn't tell you. Do you know anybody called Purzley?"

"Yes, I know a young man called Purzley—Geoffrey Purzley. He rather likes me but I don't like him much. Do you know him?"

"No," said Mark, smiling, "I hardly know anybody. Except you."

"You don't really know me," she told him, with the sudden huge solemnity of girlhood. They had stopped and were half-facing one another, in what might have been a jungle path.

He laughed again, and this time not without amusement. "In a way I know you better than you know yourself." He hesitated, wondering if he was making a fool of himself. "I can tell your fortune."

"Can you?" She was all credulity and eagerness. "How do you do it?"

"Just by looking at you. Want me to try?"

"Yes, of course. Go on, please."

After a longish stare, which he tried to make rather sinister: "You'll marry Purzley, who'll do something important and be given a title. You'll have three or four children, who will also do very well. You'll live to a ripe old age and become a most formidable old lady, striding around in old tweeds and thick shoes."

She gave an uncertain little laugh. "That's absurd. You don't know really, do you?"

He nodded. "In your case—yes, I do."

"Well, you might. Do you remember when we were all in the drawing-room, after dinner, and you talked for a minute or two to my cousin Maud and me? Well, when you left us, Maud and I were talking about you. Shall I tell you what we said? You might be flattered—or you might be furious—I don't know. But I'll risk it. Well, we agreed that there was something frightening about you. Maud said it was your eyes. I said I thought it was your manner——"

"Rude?"

"No, not really, though some people might think so. Odd— abrupt. As if you weren't English—and you are, aren't you?"

"Miss Buller, I'm very very English," he told her, with immense mock gravity.

"Now you're making fun of me. Shall we go back and see what the others are doing?"

"Yes—this time. But I warn you, it can be dangerous."

"I don't understand. What can be dangerous?"

"Going back and seeing what the others are doing." And as he followed her, at a sauntering pace, he began trying to work it out. Here, floating before him, all pink and downy, was young Dorothy Buller who in fifty years would be the old Lady Purzley who came to see what he and the others were up to with this house. Now if, when he got back (and he still refused to consider any alternative), he asked Lady Purzley if she remembered having her fortune told in this conservatory, when she was a girl, what would she reply? But wait a minute. He, Mark Denbow, couldn't possibly be part of Lady Purzley's youth, because he wasn't born then. Yet here he was with Dorothy, who undoubtedly *was* Lady Purzley round about the age of twenty. And then, trying to work it out, he was off again, just as he had been before dinner when Ronald Farspeare had left him to dress, and he had begun losing himself in a maze of time orders and dimensions. Whether he was now existing in a time quite different from that of ordinary world history, was moving in some unknown dimension where all possibilities might be realised, one sombre fact remained, that outside the immediate sense of bewilderment, like a vast dark space empty of stars, was a feeling of utter desolation, ultimate heartbreak.

The group around the piano was dispersing, but the energetic Captain Waterhouse, with the monocle still screwed into his fiery countenance, had not deserted his instrument. He began playing waltzes, dreamily at first and then, in response to several cries of encouragement, with the rhythmical emphasis of a dance pianist. Dorothy melted into the arms of a bulky young man called Archie, and was whirled away. All the ripe, soft girls, like giant peaches and plums, were soon twirling in the arms of their beefy, scarlet-faced young men. Mark loitered near the piano, seeing it all as a tiny lighted dream against the immeasurable dark.

"Now don't tell me you can't waltz," cried Maud, the middle one of the three daughters of the house. She had arrived with a footman who had brought a tray of drinks. She held up her arms invitingly, and after hesitating a moment, for it was some time since he had done any waltzing, Mark took hold of her and off they went. She was a dark, high-coloured girl, blazing with some mysterious inner excitement, passionate love or secret dreams of glory. All Mark knew about her, from the family memorial in the chapel, was that she died—or would die—in 1923, after a long illness bravely borne following upon her nursing service in Serbia. And it was not easy to dance well with a glowing creature who would soon be a long illness bravely borne and then three lines cut in marble on a chapel wall.

"I believe you hate dancing," she told him.

"Am I so bad?" He had to make an effort to find the right tone.

"Oh—no, not at all, rather good in fact. You keep good time, which most of the others don't. It's just the look on your face—in your eyes."

Pom-POM-tee-iddle-om-tiddle-om, went Captain Water-house, now happily launched into the *Valse Bleu*. Whirling and twirling and whirling the rest of them went, like the times-beyond-time, the unknown dimensions, the planets and stars.

"I've heard about my eyes already—from Dorothy Buller." And he smiled into the fiery darkness of Maud's eyes.

"Now that was jolly unfair of Dorothy," cried Maud. "I ought to have warned her—she always tells everything. But there *is* something odd and disturbing about your eyes, Mr. Denbow. Ronald never explained properly—he never does. Were you nearly drowned?"

"I'm not sure," he replied carefully. "Perhaps I was."

"That would explain it if you were," she said gravely. "As if you'd seen something we hadn't seen."

"Oh—I have—I have—I have——" he whirled her round and round, faster and faster—"lots—and lots—and lots—of things—that I couldn't—begin—to tell—you about——"

"Oh!" she cried, out of breath, "I—love this—don't you——?"

Captain Waterhouse decided that he must have a drink, while the dancers waited rather uncertainly for the music to begin again. It was then Mark noticed the girl who was standing near the door. She was an odd figure, and he knew at once that she had not been at the dinner table and that this was probably her first appearance downstairs this evening. She looked thin and ill; her dress hung badly; and there appeared to be something wrong with her hair.

"That girl over there," said Mark, "is she the one Mrs. Buller mentioned to me—Ann something—who came to the wrong house?"

"I suppose so," said Maud. "Poor darling—she does look peculiar, doesn't she? It's all rather confusing. My sister Muriel knows all about it, I don't. She's English but she's just come from France—and thought she'd been invited to stay here by some people she'd met in Paris. We think it must have been the Ferrers over at Winbone Manor—they're always going to

Paris—and I believe Muriel has sent a message to them about her. Came to the wrong house, mislaid her luggage, was half-drowned in the thunderstorm—poor girl! She wouldn't come down to dinner, had a tray upstairs, but I suppose she found it too boring staying out of sight. Though I think in her place I'd have stayed upstairs. She does look all lost and strayed, doesn't she? I wish you'd go and ask her if she'd like something to drink, and generally look after her. Will you?"

"As the other lost and strayed type," said Mark, "it's the least I can do."

"That's another thing Dorothy and I noticed," said Maud, smiling over her shoulder. "You talk in an odd way—not like anybody else we know."

As he approached her, the strange girl gave him one quick look and then never looked at him again. "Oh—well—thank you, yes I will," she cried, in what seemed almost a parody of the high girlish voices there. "Just a little lemon squash, I suppose—or something equally innocent. Shall I come with you—and see what there is?" When they reached the drinks, she said, without looking at him: "What are you going to have? And what's your name, please?"

"Mark Denbow. And you're Ann—something—aren't you?"

"I'm Ann——" and then she broke off abruptly, as if she had changed her mind about telling him her surname.

"And I am going to have some whisky," he said firmly.

The footman poured out a lemon squash for Ann while Mark helped himself to the largest whisky-and-soda he ever remembered having. This was neither greed nor desperation; the glasses were so large that they made a giant helping inevitable. It was very good whisky too. But not many of the other men were drinking it, he noticed; they were asking for brandy-and-soda. All the girls were sipping soft drinks.

"I don't like this lemon squash," cried Ann suddenly, her voice higher than ever. "Mr. Denbow, would you think me terribly wicked if I asked you to get me a whisky?"

"No." He could never see her face properly. But he saw what was wrong with her hair, which had been padded out with false hair that was not quite the same colour.

"Well, all the rest of 'em would." She giggled. "So you'd better pretend it's for yourself. Look—I'll hold your glass—and you take back this lemon stuff."

The whisky he brought her was not much smaller than the one he had given himself. "We'll go in a corner with these," she announced, and led the way. They sat on an old leather settee. There was not much light. "Nobody'll bother about us here. Or do you want somebody to bother about you?"

"No, I don't."

"Are you the one who was rescued from the lake? Yes? Well, we're a pair then. Look—they're going to dance again. Wouldn't you like to go whizzing round again with one of those jolly fat girls?"

"I'd rather stay here," said Mark. "What about you?"

"Never, never, never." She took a good long drink, and cried: "Lord—that's strong. No, no dancing for me. I can't bear any of this. Not just because I look like a freak among all these great frilly bosomy girls. It's like a sort of children's party with everybody three times the right size. I hate it."

She had stopped talking in that ridiculous high girlish voice. She turned and looked at him, so that even in that bad light he was able at last to see her face properly. And now she didn't look thin, ill, rather grotesque, she looked beautiful. For several moments, in silence, they stared at each other.

It was then that he found the first crack in this other time. As he stared at her, wondering at her beauty, everything but her face changed. They were somewhere else and—what was more important—in his own time, as he knew at once when he saw behind her the bookshelves of the school library. Just beyond her cheekbone were the green volumes of the cheap reprint of the *Cambridge Modern History*; so that he knew exactly where they were. And without looking round he knew too that Dorothy and Maud and Archie and Ronald and

Captain Waterhouse and the footman and the piano and the lighted smoke-room had vanished.

She gave a sharp exclamation. Then they were back in the old smoke-room, and Captain Waterhouse was playing a polka, and the beefy black-and-white men were taking hold of the plump pastel girls.

Her hand fastened on to his, and her sharp little nails were pressing into his palm. "Don't ask me why I'm doing this," she muttered, white-faced. "Just let me do it, there's a good kind man. I can't explain. And if I did, you wouldn't believe me."

"Yes, I would. Because I can explain too."

"No, you can't," she said crossly. "And don't start being clever and showing off. Just be a comfort—or leave me alone."

He grinned at her, and then indicated the prancing girls, billowing in their full skirts. "*They* wouldn't talk to me like that. And you shouldn't."

"Right both times," she said gloomily. She had wonderful dark hazel eyes; and the delicate yet strong moulding of her face, with its wide cheekbones and hollows beneath, was a joy. "They wouldn't talk like that—and I oughtn't to. You were kind too. I apologise." She jumped up. "But I can't stand any more of this. I'm going."

She was running out of the room while he was still pushing himself out of the deep settee. It was no use running after her. These people were fairly free-and-easy but they might be annoyed if they saw the two interlopers running round the house. Perching himself on the end of the settee, he watched the dancers. They were there all right, solidly there, with nothing shadowy about them, all real people; but if they had been dolls performing a polka he could not have felt further removed from them. And now the feeling of desolation returned. It had left him, he realised now, while he had been with the girl Ann.

Just as he had decided to go and find her, if she were still somewhere downstairs, the dancing stopped and the next moment Ronald and Dorothy Buller were barring his way.

"It's no use, Denbow," said Ronald, smiling, "she won't stop talking about you."

"I only said you told fortunes," said Dorothy. "And Ronnie's dying to have his told, but won't admit it."

"If Denbow will tell my fortune, I'll be delighted," cried Ronald. "What about it, old man?" Of all the young men there, he was the most dazzling: golden-haired, pink-skinned, and with the bright blue eyes of a happy baby. He made the girls, for all their opulence, look dim and dowdy. Looking at him, Mark wondered if those stupid battles of the First World War, like that of Neuve Chapelle which would blot Ronald from this earth, had not destroyed for ever this vivid and even gorgeous masculine type. Although some Americans, in their own way, resembled it.

"Who's he going to marry?" cried Dorothy, while Mark still hesitated. "I'll bet you know, or think you do, just as you did with me—though of course you're all wrong about Geoffrey Purzley. Too absurd. But please—go on, tell him. Marriage first."

"You girls and your marriages," said Ronald, fingering his golden moustache. But he looked expectantly at Mark.

"I don't know," said Mark unhappily. "I believe you will marry—but I don't know who it is. Sorry!"

"Are you feeling all right, Denbow?" asked Ronald.

"No, you're not, are you?" said Dorothy, anxious now. She was staring hard at him, with a flicker almost of fear in her eyes.

"I feel—a bit peculiar," said Mark carefully. But he knew in fact that something odd was happening. It was as if the years were coming between him and them like a sort of thickening of the air, in which all colour was draining away and shapes losing their sharp edge. Their voices were still clear enough, but they seemed to be coming from further away.

"Better turn in, old man," Ronald was saying. "Like me to give you a hand? Or I can ask one of the servants to show you up to your room."

"No, thank you," said Mark. "I think I'm finding it rather hot in here. I'll take a turn outside. Excuse me."

As he slowly crossed the room, he heard the piano again behind him, starting another waltz, but its tinkle was far away, like that of a piano heard distantly in the night. He turned at the door, for a last look at the dancers, suddenly convinced that he would never see them again. There was no colour at all in the scene now. They were shadows waltzing, to the tiny ghost of a tune. . . . .

He made his way along a corridor to the large front hall, and there he saw the old butler preparing to bolt the great doors. "Just a minute," he cried, hurrying forward. "I want to go out."

The old man never looked up but reached down towards another bolt. Probably he was deaf.

"No, hold it," cried Mark, now nearly at his elbow.

But the last bolts went home. The butler slowly straightened himself and then turned a complete blank face to Mark, who was not more than two feet away from him. And Mark realised that the man could neither see nor hear him. So far as this butler was concerned, he no longer existed—or rather had not come into existence. Yet the hall to Mark was still the hall of a night in 1902, had not yet turned itself back again into the hall he knew so well.

He stayed there a few minutes after the butler had gone, wondering what to do. One thing he felt fairly certain about, that this evening of 1902, into which he had dived so inexplicably, would not last much longer for him. Already he himself had ceased to be a visible presence in the scene, and at any moment now, he felt, it might disappear from his sight and hearing, as it had done when he had suddenly seen Ann, for a few seconds, against the background of the school library. When he had seen her, in fact, in his own time, not in this other time. And did this mean that she was in his own time? He had already guessed she was, just after she had demanded some whisky and had talked as if she had made this time-jump too.

He began wondering if she too were now invisible to these people of fifty years ago. He decided to go in search of her.

He found her in the large drawing-room, sitting stiffly at the edge of a group of the older people. Although she was taking no part in the talk, he was certain that the others were clearly aware of her and that she was still part of the scene. He was equally certain that nobody there was aware of him, not even Ann. But unlike the others, who never gave a glance in his direction when he arrived near them, Ann knew that something had happened. As he came near he saw a look of bewilderment cross her face. But he knew she had not actually seen him.

All the older and important guests seemed to be there: a politician, some general, a wealthy industrialist, a bleached old gnome of a banker; and Lord Broxwood himself, massive and purple, was with them, a sort of chairman. They were important and weighty men, and spoke of important and weighty affairs—the state of the country, of Europe, of the world, and the future of the country, of Europe, of the world. They were men of experience, they were experts in one field or another; so they made pontifical announcements, and without hesitation, unshadowed by any doubt, they produced their solemn prophecies, to the accompaniment of approving grunts and nods. Until Ann jumped up, fiery-eyed and rather shrill, and made her speech.

"I know this seems horribly rude and that you'll all be furious," she cried, "but I can't help it. Please listen for once—and stop being so grand and thinking you know everything. I've listened to you, haven't I? All about what's going to happen here in England, and what France will do to Italy and Russia to Germany and all that——"

"Really, Miss—er——" Lord Broxwood began, turning a deeper shade of purple with annoyance. "I don't think——"

But Ann could not be stopped. "I know, I know. Who am I—and all that. But please—please—listen for once. I shan't take long. But I must warn you that you're all talking nonsense. It may weigh a ton but it's all just rubbish, bilge and rot. I know roughly what's going to happen during these next fifty years—never mind how, but I do—and I can assure you that it's all quite different from what you think. Nothing you've said is going to come true. Honestly it isn't. You're all miles and miles out. So you just might as well stop thinking you know it all, because you haven't a clue. Not one of you—not a clue. It's pathetic. And I'll never believe people like you again. Well, I *am* shutting up."

This final remark was addressed to Lord Broxwood, who at the risk of giving himself a fit of apoplexy was now lumbering forward, apparently ready to shut her up by force. Before he could reach her, Ann had turned and, finding herself facing an open french window, had bolted into the night. Mark hurried after her, followed her across the lawn, and finally caught up with her inside the old summer house. She was crying.

"Leave me alone," she mumbled, hearing him but not looking up. "I know I was damned rude—but you don't understand."

"Yes, I do," said Mark. "I'm just the one who does."

There was very little light in there but it was not quite dark. She looked up, though it was probably his voice she recognised. "Oh—it's you again." She sounded much relieved. Indeed, he felt hopefully, she sounded almost delighted.

"You can see me now?" he asked.

"Not very well of course, but I can see that it's you. Why?"

"You couldn't see me in that drawing-room."

"Were you there?"

"Yes. But nobody knew."

"I felt that somebody came in," she said, rather eagerly. "But I'll admit I didn't really see you. You heard me, then?"

"You said just what I wanted to say." Mark was enthusiastic. "But I doubt if I'd have had the guts to say it."

She came closer, stared through the dark into his face, put out a hand and pressed it into the lapel of his coat, as if to make sure he was solid and real. "You're not one of them—are you?

I wondered before, when you got me the whisky. But then I thought there couldn't be two of us. Oh—you've changed your suit."

"Why—no—I——" But then he felt the familiar soft collar round his neck, and one quick movement of a hand told him he was wearing his tweed coat and corduroy trousers.

"And I've changed my clothes—thank God!" she cried. "And look! Isn't the light from that drawing-room different?"

It was the usual light that came from the main recreation room any night the students were using it. Before he knew what to say to her, they were crossing the lawn towards the uncurtained french windows. Above the confused sounds of voices and a subdued samba on the gramophone, they could hear the clatter of table-tennis balls.

"Do you have tournaments?" asked Ann in an easy offhand way.

"Yes," he told her. "They're probably playing in one tonight."

Then he drew in his breath sharply, noisily. How could she be standing there with him, looking through the window at the students, and asking a question in that tone, as if she had already asked scores of questions and he was showing her round the school? As if she had never been back fifty years? As if neither of them had been back?

"What's the matter, Mr. Denbow?" she enquired innocently. "Are you cold? Shall we go in—back to the library?"

"Why yes—I think we might as well." He heard himself saying this, remotely from all the questions buzzing in his mind.

Not wishing to disturb the students, they walked round to the side door and along the back corridor towards the library. He said nothing, not knowing what to say, still trying to understand what had happened. She was walking half a pace ahead of him, so that he could look at her without appearing ill-mannered. A mop of soft dark hair; a figure, now trimly clothed, as delicate and strong as her face; yes, a beautiful girl, typical of the best of our time. But what about that other time? Didn't she know she had been there?

They had the corridor to themselves. Within a few feet of the library door, she stopped and turned on him. "Mr. Denbow, I like what you're doing here," she began, with a touch of severity, "though I thought I wouldn't. And I'm ready to like you. But I feel you resent me—and I think that's terribly unfair. I'm not my grandmother, you know."

"I'm sorry if I've behaved as if I thought you were your grandmother," said Mark, without a clue to what they were talking about. "And I've never met anybody I felt less like resenting. But let's talk about this in the library."

"In front of my grandmother? Surely that wouldn't be a good idea. That's why I stopped here."

"Oh—your grandmother's in the library—is she?" Mark stared at her blankly.

"Well, that's where we left her," said Ann impatiently. Then she looked at him curiously. "You don't look very good. Perhaps that little accident in the lake was worse than you thought——"

"Just a minute," said Mark earnestly, going closer and lowering his voice. "Please tell me something. Have I been showing you round this place——?"

"But of course—for the last hour. Then we went out for some air, and then you said you'd better take an aspirin and I said I'd wait for you in the old summer house—you remember?"

"This is terribly important." And he found himself gripping her just below each shoulder. "Tell me, please, what happened to you while you waited in the summer house. It doesn't matter how absurd it seems—please tell me."

"Well—I had a confused sort of day-dream—I'm a dreamy type though I may not look it. By the way, you're hurting my arms—but go on, if it helps. No—no apologies. I can see this is serious for you. You see, on the way here—perhaps you don't remember, but my grandmother and I are staying with some

people called Ferrers at Winbone Manor, and I wanted to drive
over, so she came with me—well, on the way here she was
telling me how she used to stay here as a girl—she was the
niece of the Lord Broxwood who owned it then. So I began
imagining what it would be like here in those days—oh!" And
she stared at him, as if she had suddenly remembered something.

"Ann," he whispered desperately, "I'm going to take a
chance and say this now. Don't think I'm mad. I'm not. But
I tell you I spent most of this evening there—in 1902, it was.
And you were the strange girl who'd turned up in some queer
way, just as I'd been rescued from the lake—by the son of the
house, a chap called Ronald. Then I saw how beautiful you
were—yes, the most beautiful girl I'd ever known. And I knew
you didn't belong to that time but to this. There were just the
two of us in a different world that didn't understand. And I've
never been really in love before, and I know this is it—and that
whatever happens you'll always be the beautiful strange girl
who turns out not to be strange but really the other one in
a different world that couldn't understand. That's how it'll
always be, whatever happens. Do I sound quite mad?"

"Yes," said Ann. "But I like it. Though of course there's a lot
more you'll have to tell me."

The library door opened. "Don't stand there looking
moonstruck," cried a sharp old voice. "Either come in or go
somewhere else."

He felt he ought to have known at once that this grandmother would be Lady Purzley—once Dorothy Buller,
bosomy and downy in pink.

"If you two were talking about adult education out there,"
said Lady Purzley, after examining their looks critically, "then I
no longer understand anything."

"Yes, you do, darling," cried Ann, still glowing away. "But it
was a kind of adult education."

"I must say," said the old lady, turning to Mark, "you're a
more enterprising young man than I thought you were."

"I'm far more enterprising than I thought I was," said Mark, smiling at her. "By the way, Lady Purzley, when you stayed here as a girl, did a strange young man ever tell your fortune in the conservatory?"

"Now why should you ask me that, Mr. Denbow?"

"I just wondered."

"Because," Lady Purzley continued slowly, "I dozed a little after you two left me, and dreamt I was back here as a girl, before I was even engaged to Geoffrey Purzley, and somebody told me I would marry him. But whether that really happened once or I merely dreamt it, I can't remember. It's often difficult to tell, you know. Things can be very complicated."

"So I've suspected," said Mark.

THE STATUES

WALTER VOLEY was a reporter on the *Daily Record*, and one of its best men. He had been with the paper fifteen years, coming to it from a suburban weekly; and now he was given many of the more important London stories and often had a by-line. He lived fairly comfortably in a Northern suburb, had a pleasant wife and a promising son, at whom he grumbled, and a lazy impudent daughter, whom he adored. He was a fattish man in his late forties, smoked a pipe all day, and had trouble with his digestion.

In his youth he had been happy enough, but now, though outwardly cheerful, he was anything but happy. Sometimes for days together he would travel from his home to the office, dodge about central London chasing down his stories, go back to the office and write his stuff, have a drink or two with some of the boys, hurry home to eat supper and then potter about, all in a fixed mood of melancholy bewilderment. It is of course a state of mind well-known to many men in their forties, when they are no longer young and hopeful and yet have not reached the resignation of age. The trouble with Voley was that his job compelled him to live in a world crackling with excitement and he no longer felt any excitement himself. He still pretended both in and out of print that he was at least as excited as anybody else, but inside he felt glum and puzzled. A Hollywood star, whose marriage was breaking up, arrived in town; a Cabinet Minister had made a reckless statement; the flat of a well-known actress had been broken into; youth in West London was misbehaving itself; an important announcement was about to be made by the Television chief: *So what?* cried Voley to himself. Sometimes he felt he had been on this merry-go-round too long. Perhaps a change of job would help. At other times, especially when his digestion was playing him up, he wondered in despair what sense and satisfaction there could be in all this fuss and running around and 'phoning and wiring and rushing into print under large headlines. What was it all about? Was this really life, all that could reasonably be expected of it, or was it a bad imitation that had somehow been foisted on to him? And there were moments when he asked himself if the Press, which had to discover so much false excitement every morning, had to manufacture crises and crimes at a pinch, did not do more harm than good. But his dissatisfaction extended to other people's lives, of which he saw a good deal in his professional capacity, as well as darkening his own. The rush hours, the housing misery, the anxiety about money, the rat-race for cushy jobs! How often did you see among all these crowds one smooth calm face, eyes that were bright but not greedy?

It was towards the end of a glittering morning in April that he saw the first statue. He was on top of a bus in the Bayswater Road, going towards Marble Arch. He had been to a smelly basement in Notting Hill, interviewing a woman who was preparing to claim a fortune and who was almost an idiot. He was smoking his pipe and assembling in his mind what was left of this fortune-claiming story when he happened to glance at the park. And there it was, far higher than any trees, an immense figure, looking as if it might have been cast in pale bronze. For a few seconds, while he still remained sitting there, astounded, he could see its features, which of course were of enormous size. It was a male figure, but the face was not like that of any man Voley had ever seen: it was noble and serene, but strange, as if belonging to some unknown race. He saw it all quite clearly, standing there in the white sunlight of spring. What was it doing there? Who had put it up? How had the *Record* missed the story? But while he was asking himself these questions, he was hurrying down from the top of the bus and then impatiently waiting for it to stop.

He arrived in the park almost fighting for his breath. He saw at once, although he tried to pretend that the light was playing tricks, that no such statue existed there. He dodged about for a few minutes, but of course there was nothing. The absurdity of the hallucination then struck him. Why, a thing that size, probably at least eighty feet high, would have taken weeks, perhaps months, to erect, and all London would have been talking about it and there would have been scores of columns in the *Record* and all the other papers. What a fine reporter he was, to imagine anything else! Well, was there a story here? He told himself firmly there was not. He had been day-dreaming, and there was no point in advertising the fact. Walter Voley and his giant statue! Chump!

"A funny thing happened to me this morning," he began, at the supper table that night. But too many funny things had happened to other members of his family, who had more enthusiasm or determination than he had. Afterwards he was glad that he had not persisted in telling them. The memory of the statue had not faded as something seen in a dream would probably have done. If he closed his eyes and made an effort he could still see that gigantic bronze face, high above the park, looking towards the West. Its nobility and serenity seemed to linger in his mind, like a taste of sweetness on the tongue. Long after he ought to have been asleep, he was still brooding over that statue, asking himself futile questions about it. If it was part of a day-dream, how had he contrived to plant it so neatly in the very section of the park the bus was passing? Why should the statue be there and everything else, so far as he could remember, look normal? How had he been able to *invent* a thing like that, so majestic, so strange? He found it difficult to believe he had invented it. Hadn't he felt almost at once that it belonged to some unknown race?

For the next two weeks he went about his work, for all the attention it demanded, lost in a sad dream. It was harder now to recapture his glimpse of the great statue, but somehow the atmosphere of its presence remained with him. He felt it was there somewhere, calmly gazing at the Western sky, while he himself and all his concerns were smaller, fussier and more ridiculous than ever. Again and again he asked himself, with increasing despair, what sort of life this was that he should fling his days into it as if it were an incinerator and his time were rubbish to be burnt. For the first few days he tried to avoid the Bayswater side of the park, fearing to be disappointed, but during the second week he went out of his way several times to have another look. And of course it was not there.

Then he saw another one. It was late in a cloudy afternoon, threatening rain. He had been to see a man in the City and was walking back to the office. At Ludgate Circus he happened to look up to the right, and there, where Holborn Viaduct ought to have been but was not, was another giant statue. This was quite different: it was even larger than the first, but apparently carved out of some black substance, and represented a powerful naked man agonisingly attempting to free himself from something that gripped him. For a couple of seconds or so, it was there, clear and distinct and appallingly impressive; and then, long before the lights had changed and Voley was able to cross the road, it had vanished, and the old Viaduct was back. He knew this time that it was useless to go nearer the place where the statue ought to have been; so he walked slowly on, carrying an image of the struggling figure, the huge dark features twisted with a sense of effort and pain. And as he went he told himself that although the two statues were so dissimilar, they belonged to the same age, the same people, whatever and whoever they might be.

"You're a bit down, aren't you, Walter?" said Fryson, the sports editor, later that day over a drink. "Don't you like this rain?"

"Not much," said Voley, "but that's not it. Now just keep this to yourself, will you? I'm seeing things that aren't there, and that nobody else sees. No," he added hastily, "I can't say that. For all I know, other people may see them, and be keeping quiet about it, just as I've done up to now. No, I know—you don't know what I'm talking about. Keep calm. But the fact is,

Arthur, twice now I've seen huge statues." And he described them both, together with the circumstances in which he had seen them.

"Well," said Fryson, who to Voley's relief did not try to be facetious about the statues, "if you ask me, Walter, I'd say that the first time you were feeling drowsy in the bus—I often nod off myself—and dreamt you saw a statue in the park. Then the next time you made it up, after thinking about the other one so often. You began to expect to see another, so you did."

"I'd agree with you," said Voley earnestly, "if these statues were like ours, only bigger. But they aren't, you know. They aren't our sort of statue. They look like a different kind of people. They don't belong to us at all. If I'd made them up, they couldn't look so strange."

"Sure you're all right, Walter?"

"I'm not going barmy, if that's what you mean. But I'm not sure I'm all right, or that you're all right, or that anybody we know round here is all right. I've been uncertain about that for some time, and these statues have made it seem worse. Arthur," he concluded gravely, "we couldn't have put up those things. We haven't it in us."

"I can think of a lot of things I'd want before I'd ask for statues eighty to a hundred feet high. Waste of materials and labour, I'd say."

"Not if you'd seen them you wouldn't, Arthur. I know I didn't see them long——"

"If you saw them at all——"

"I *thought* I saw them, and that's enough," cried Voley with a flash of impatience. "And the point is that although I didn't see them long, they weren't just objects, something to stare at and then ignore. They *meant* something—though don't ask me what—and you couldn't be indifferent to them. I have an idea you wouldn't feel the same if they were always about. And as for wasting materials and labour, what do you think we're doing all the time? Cutting down whole forests just to print a lot of damned tripe——"

"Here, steady, somebody might be listening."

"But you know what I mean, Arthur."

"As a matter of fact, I do, Walter. But I'm not in favour of these statues, and if I were you, I'd stop seeing 'em. When are you taking your holiday this year?"

"Early September, with luck. But don't get funny ideas about me, old man, and remember—keep this to yourself."

"I will," said Fryson. "But take it easy a bit. We don't want one of our best old war-horses seeing things that aren't there."

He said nothing at home, and several times both his wife and his daughter told him he was becoming absent-minded in his old age. Once indeed his wife demanded to know what was wrong, and clearly suspected some trouble on the *Record* that he was hiding from her. And although he assured her there was no trouble, it was a fact that recently several fairly good assignments he had been given had not turned out too well. He had missed what was thought to be a good angle or had turned in copy that read like stale re-hashing. He had had to admit that he was at fault. What he could not say in extenuation was that London without the statues, the *real* London (though often it seemed completely unreal, a place in a muddled, squalid dream), hardly appeared worth writing about. Now if the statues were really there, what a story he could write!

The third, and the last he saw in any detail, came towards the end of May, after he had returned to the office about seven in the evening, to write a story he had been chasing round all day. The *Daily Record* building is in one of those short streets that run between Fleet Street and the Embankment, and from the reporters' room, which is high up, you can look down to your left and see the river. Having rather wearily delivered his copy, he was standing by one of the windows, filling his pipe and wondering whether to eat a late supper at home or go along to the Club. It was nearly sunset and there was a golden bloom outside the windows. He looked idly towards the river, and then he saw it. This statue must have been white in clear daylight but at that moment it was cream and gold. It was of great size, the largest of the three, and of extraordinary beauty, making his heart leap almost in pain. A majestic but smiling woman, apparently clothed in a simple long robe, held up a naked laughing child. For a few moments he saw every detail of the vast carving, from the hem of the robe, around which the river was winking and flashing, right up to the child's curls gilded by the sun.

"God Almighty!" he cried, rapt and breathless.

"Now what is it, Pop?" This was from a young woman called Aiken, who did fashion and social stuff. "Something happening on the river?" And she joined him at the window.

"A pleasing peep at Old Father Thames," she told him, "but nothing to get excited about. And I must go, because I *have* something to get excited about, with any luck. What's the matter, Mr. Voley?"

"Gone now," he muttered. "Can't explain. You wouldn't believe me. Something I saw."

"A mirage? Elizabeth One on her way to Greenwich or wherever it was she spoke her piece about the Armada? Tell me—but like lightning because I must certainly go."

Voley shook his head. "You've been at college fairly recently, Miss Aiken. Now tell me—has there ever been a city, a country, where there were gigantic statues—oh—a hundred feet high?"

"Why? Oh—all right, there isn't time. Well—India perhaps and all points East of that. No? How about Ancient Egypt? They went in for statuary on a big scale. Try the Library. And tell me all about it next time."

He did not tell her, and indeed she never asked, but he did surprise old Saunders in the Library by asking him for photographs and drawings of ancient Egyptian statues. But a glance told him these were quite unlike the three statues he had seen.

"Do you think London ever had statues as big as these Egyptian things?" he asked Saunders.

"I'm sure it didn't. Why, Mr. Voley?"

"Well," he hesitated, "this sounds silly—but I assure you

it's no joke. I've been seeing some enormous statues—three altogether. Just for half a minute I see them quite plainly—and then they vanish. Wonderful things they are. I'm certain I couldn't imagine them. And if I'm not, then what is it I'm seeing?"

"Some people are supposed to be able to see the Past," said Saunders slowly. "I suppose that was in your mind—humph?"

"More or less," Voley replied vaguely. "Something like second sight. Though I can tell you, Mr. Saunders, nobody ever fancied himself less at that sort of thing than I do."

"On the other hand," said Saunders, eyeing Voley in a calmly speculative fashion, "you might be seeing the Future——"

"Here—steady!" cried Voley.

"Having a glimpse or two of London," the other continued, "as it will be in five hundred or a thousand years' time."

"But how can I see statues that won't come into existence for hundreds of years?"

"Perhaps they're already existing *somewhere*—that is, somewhere in Time. We have a book or two on that subject and I've read them—very complicated and rather far-fetched, but enjoyable. Like to have a go at one, Mr. Voley?"

"Not just now, Mr. Saunders, thank you."

Things were bad enough, he decided, without entangling himself in fantastic theories that he could never understand. And indeed this glimpse of the third and most impressive statue made him feel much worse than he had done before. It was as if more than half of him had been captured by that other London where the statues were. What had seemed merely futile in his work and life now seemed intolerable. He moved about like a man caught by and then fixed in a squalid and idiotic dream. The *Record* itself and the world it reflected seemed to him now not worth an hour of a real man's time. He did not feel any better at home. He felt cut off from his wife and children, although he loved them dearly. He could not mention the statues to them now, no longer made any attempt to describe his experiences. His wife seemed perfectly at ease and content in this world from which he was drifting. If his children grumbled, it was because they wanted a larger share of this world, more *Record* stuff and not less of it. When he tried to visit the statues in imagination, he could not see his family with him; and this he found hateful. He was a bewildered unhappy man, and at home they knew it, so that he sometimes caught them exchanging knowing or pitying glances, and at work the men closest to him had begun to guess there was something wrong.

The climax came at Mr. Bleck's annual cocktail party for the *Record* editorial and reporting staff. Mr. Bleck was the managing editor and had a fine house, with quite a garden, in Highgate Village. It had a flat roof and Mr. Bleck liked to take people up there and show them all London gleaming and smouldering below. After a few drinks, Voley made one of a small party who were taken up there. It was about half-past six on a glorious Saturday in early June.

"I know some of you have seen it before," cried Mr. Bleck, who had had a few drinks too, "but it'll do you no harm to take another look. Finest view of London I know. If there's a better one, tell me where it is." And he waved a hand possessively, as if he had made it all.

Voley had been up there before, and admired the view nearly as much as Mr. Bleck did. But this time he was not thinking about it, for the drinks he had had, much stronger than the glasses of bitter he usually had early in the evening, had somehow brought him closer to the statues and all that he thought and felt about them, and had made the party, for all its colour and noise, seem almost like something in a day-dream. But like the others, he went to the rail along the parapet, and stared down at the vast sprawl of the city.

All the three statues he had seen before were there, clearly recognisable, and there were scores of others, whose exact shape and character he could not distinguish at that distance. And these giant figures rose out of a city that was almost entirely unfamiliar, for nearly every big building he had seen before from that roof had vanished, the whole lay-out of the city was different, and only the river and the larger parks were the same. It was London all right, but no London that he had ever seen before or ever would see except in such a moment as this. He had just time for one good look at it, during which it was quite clear and distinct in the sunlight, and then the great statues and the strange buildings and avenues misted over and faded and vanished. The city he had hurried about in for so many years sullenly returned, waiting for him to report its meaningless events. He gave a loud cry of despair, out of an interior darkness.

They called it a nervous breakdown, and it was many months before he was fit to work again. Then at his own request, after much argument at home, sometimes hopeful, sometimes bitter, he was transferred to a provincial paper controlled by the *Daily Record* group, the *Burmanley Evening Record*, for which he still reports Council meetings, Industrial Fairs, fêtes and bazaars, a quiet, ageing man who says little and has a trick of staring in bewilderment at nothing.

THE LEADINGTON INCIDENT

THE TRAIN was quieter now. This was the moment, Cobthorn thought. He leaned forward and turned to knock the ash off his cigar. "As a matter of fact," he said, still looking at the ashtray, "I happen to be the Minister in charge of that particular department."

"Are you indeed?" said the man. There was nothing more than the merest politeness in his tone. Either he was not impressed or he was putting up an impudent bluff. He was a plumpish fellow with a large pale face, about as distinguished as the crumpled suit he was wearing. He was English, Cobthorn had decided, and might be a professional man or a civil servant on the assistant-secretary level. Whatever he was, he certainly did not look as if he met Cabinet Ministers every day.

"Yes. I'm Sir George Cobthorn." And he stared rather hard across the compartment, still bright with the afternoon sun. He knew he had not been able to announce himself without a touch of self-importance, and this increased his irritation. Just because he had finished his notes for tonight's speech, he told himself, he need not have begun an unrewarding talk with this fellow.

The man merely nodded. He had no fussy mannerisms and appeared never to waste any energy on unnecessary movements and words, a characteristic that Cobthorn had never been able to acquire. Another reason why the man was so irritating.

"We're holding a big meeting tonight in Leadington," Cobthorn heard himself announcing. "I'm making a rather important statement of policy."

The man smiled and nodded again.

"I can't anticipate that statement, of course," Cobthorn continued, determined now to arouse some interest, "but I don't mind telling you that it represents a change of policy that—er—will make a good deal of difference to all our lives. As the Press will be telling us tomorrow." And he produced that wide friendly grin which almost automatically followed any reference he ever made to the Press.

The man smiled, again out of mere politeness. And Cobthorn knew that if he had told him he proposed to keep a few fowls or had bought a new set of tyres for his car, the fellow's reaction would have been the same. There was no escaping the fact—in this fellow's opinion what Cobthorn said or did *was not important at all.*

Really this was infuriating. Cobthorn wished he had kept quiet, but now that the damage was done—for an injury to his *morale* might conceivably affect his speech tonight—he felt he must come out of this encounter with some victory on his side. Moreover, the fellow deserved a snub.

"I'm afraid I'm boring you," said Cobthorn with savage irony. "We political chaps are apt to forget there are still some people who prefer not to trouble themselves about their country's affairs." And he ended with a short sarcastic laugh. Not a very adult performance, he realised, but something had to be done.

The man seemed to be looking at him from a great distance. This calm remote regard made Cobthorn feel small, fussy, foolish. Which was intolerable as well as being plainly unreasonable. After all he was George Cobthorn, a member of Her Majesty's Government, responsible for a vast public department, a familiar figure to millions. Who was this fellow? Well, that was the line to take.

"Are you—er—a native of Leadington?" Cobthorn enquired, with a touch of patronage.

"No, I am like you," came the reply, smilingly. "I am going there to address a meeting. Only—it is not a big meeting but a very small meeting. Perhaps six people."

This was more like it. "Ah!—we'll do better than that, I fancy, in the old Beaconsfield Hall. With luck, probably between two and three thousand."

This time the other did not smile but merely nodded, gave Cobthorn a sharp look, then picked up his book.

"No comments?" demanded Cobthorn, with an edge on his voice.

"Must I make a comment?" It was more annoying than deliberate rudeness. As if a patient adult were addressing a child.

Cobthorn was tired, for he had been kept in the House the previous night, and he was anxious about tonight's meeting; so he found his temper hard to control. "Really, my dear sir," he began explosively, "it doesn't matter to me whether you make any comment or not. Only I find your attitude rather strange in an educated man. These are difficult times, you know. We're faced with some very urgent problems."

"We are indeed," said the man mildly. "But you and I may not be facing the same problems. What may seem important to you may seem of no importance to me."

"Possibly." Cobthorn was aggressive. "But I hope—for all our sakes—you are not going to tell your meeting that. Better abandon it and come to mine." He gave a short sarcastic laugh again.

Already the mills and warehouses of Leadington were cutting off some of the daylight, and the train was reducing speed. In a few minutes they would be there. No need to say any more. Cobthorn began fastening his dispatch case. Then he stood up.

The other man was standing too, and now their eyes met on this new level, at much closer range. Cobthorn did not propose to be out-stared; he was used to handling all sorts of men. But he found himself blinking; there was something curiously luminous about this fellow's stare. The carriage was darker of course, for now Leadington's grimy station was closing round them.

"These six people I hope to talk to," the man was saying, "are at least struggling to be alive."

"So are the two or three thousand I shall talk to," Cobthorn heard himself saying.

"I am afraid not," said the other quite calmly. "Most people in Leadington, like most people elsewhere, are either asleep or dead."

Cobthorn had meant to turn away, to reach for his bag, but this pronouncement was really too much. "That seems to me a most stupid and arrogant statement," he cried angrily. And then tried to turn away but found that he couldn't.

"Very well," came the voice, as if remotely from behind the stare that was now a luminous haze. "You will see."

And then they were in the station, and by the time Cobthorn had taken down his bag, hat and light overcoat, the man had gone. Clearly he was some sort of crank, probably earning a dubious and seedy living going about the country talking nonsense to little groups of fellow cranks. He might too, in order to further his hocus-pocus, have developed some hypnotic trick, with that luminous stare. Cobthorn made an impatient sound as he put his things together. He would see, would he? Well, it served him right for wasting his time chattering to the fellow when he ought to have been reading his notes.

"Porter, sir?" It came in the thick Leadington accent.

"Yes, take this bag and coat. I'll carry the dispatch case."

And then—an extraordinary coincidence, and one that would make a good story out of this encounter—he noticed that the porter, an oldish man, really did look as if he were moving in a trance. You could in fact not unreasonably have described him as being asleep. Not altogether astonishing, though. Too many of these fellows nowadays *were* half asleep, a fact that explained many of our economic problems. It might be worth while saying as much somewhere at the beginning of his speech. A good Press quote there, possibly a headline.

Two or three photographers were on the platform, waiting

for him, and with them a small group, in which he recognised, after a moment, old Douglas Jerdan, the local Party chairman, and Morrow, the agent for the Leadington area and one of the best of the Party's provincial men. Before he had time to exchange more than half-a-dozen words with old Jerdan, they were photographed together; then he had to say something to the reporters, not a bright bunch; and it was not until they had gone across to the Midland Hotel, where a suite had been booked for him, that he had any chance of properly observing Jerdan and Morrow.

But then it came in one horrible flash, just as they were settling down in his sitting-room. Old Jerdan was not merely old and foolish—*he was dead*. Probably he had been dead for years. Of course he could still move and speak—as soon as he stopped moving and speaking he would be laid out and buried—nevertheless, as Cobthorn saw quite clearly, he was dead.

After making this shocking discovery, Cobthorn found it difficult to talk to old Jerdan, and after fumbling around for something to say, he turned to Morrow, whom he remembered as a smart little agent and organiser.

"I hear you're making a good job of the local organisations," he said. "They were talking about you the other day at Central Office. All bouquets—no brickbats!"

"That's what I like to hear, Sir George," said Morrow. "But I'm lucky up here—got some very useful keen types."

"How's it looking for the meeting tonight?"

"Couldn't be better, Sir George. All the tickets gone for the area seats and front circle, and my stewards are expecting a nice crowd even up in the gallery. Just been round to test the mike and speakers and to make sure the platform looks all right."

"Not been overdoing it, have you, Morrow?" enquired Cobthorn, frowning at him.

"Who—me? In one sense I suppose I'm always overdoing it," said Morrow, "because I start in the morning and generally finish round about midnight. But I'm feeling fine. Why, Sir George?"

Cobthorn did not know what to reply to that. You cannot tell a man, especially a keen, smart fellow like Morrow, that he seems to be asleep. It was not that the usual keenness and smartness were missing; they were there all right; but they seemed to belong to a man who was talking and gesticulating in his sleep.

"I don't know what we'd do now without Morrow here." This came from Jerdan. But the remark did not bring old Jerdan back to life. No, he was dead. And Morrow was asleep.

Any sitting-room in the Midland Hotel, Leadington, is a perfect setting for a chat with a dead man and a somnambulist. Cobthorn glanced round the chill and melancholy apartment, and fortunately caught sight of a bell. "What about a drink?" he cried with false heartiness. "A little early perhaps, but I had a late night at the House. No, I'll ring. What will you have?"

The waiter who took his order was a very young man, who appeared to have just arrived from some Eastern Mediterranean country. He also appeared to be soundly asleep. Like Morrow, his eyes were open and he moved easily enough; but Cobthorn knew at once that he was asleep.

"Now—listen to me," cried Cobthorn, after he had given the order. "I don't want you to bring these drinks—never mind why, but I don't. Tell them to send some other waiter."

"Something wrong with that chap, Sir George?" asked Morrow, when the young waiter had gone.

"Yes, if you must know." Cobthorn was curt. "Seemed to me more than half asleep."

"Lots of these fellows are nowadays," old Jerdan muttered, still dead.

"Plenty of life in Leadington, though," said Morrow, without any sign of waking up himself. "I've been surprised."

"Well, I hope I'll be surprised," Cobthorn heard himself growling. He was beginning to take a sharp dislike to the place.

A few minutes later the surprise arrived. It arrived with the waiter who brought the drinks. He was an elderly man, careful and slow in his movements but still bright-eyed. And, to Cobthorn's instant relief, he was both alive and awake.

"That's better," cried Cobthorn, as if welcoming the drinks.

But it was not better. The next moment, as the waiter presented the bill to be signed, Cobthorn felt at once that this old fellow was much too alive and awake. There was mocking knowledge in his bright glance, which seemed to say "Yes, I'm all right, but how many more are you going to find like me—alive and awake?" Somehow he knew that old Jerdan was dead and Morrow was asleep, and knew that Cobthorn knew.

Cobthorn had to say something to him, the first thing that came into his head. "Are you going to be on duty later tonight?"

"No, sir. I go off at seven." The tone was respectful, all that it should be, and yet the mocking knowledge was still there.

"Better come to our meeting then," Cobthorn told him, in a big, bluff, V.I.P. manner. "Beaconsfield Hall at eight. It may turn out to be quite an occasion. I'm saying one or two rather important things."

"I'm sure you are, sir," said the waiter smoothly, his glance veiled now. "But I'm not free tonight. A little group of us meet once a month——"

"You do, do you?" cried Cobthorn, bluffer than ever. "And what d'you talk about—Communism?"

"Oh no, sir!" And suddenly the man opened his eyes wide, and Cobthorn felt idiotically that he had seen them before. "Something very different, sir. Will there be anything else? Thank *you*, sir."

Cobthorn was glad to see him go and yet felt horribly deflated once he had gone. The drinks did not waken Morrow or bring old Jerdan back to life. Cobthorn made an effort, talked about the Party, told them what the P.M. had said to him the day before, gave them two funny stories about the Leader of the Opposition. This passed the time until the drinks were finished, but even when the other two were laughing they still seemed dead or asleep. Finally, Cobthorn produced a yawn or two, and they left, promising that he would not be disturbed until quarter of an hour before the meeting.

He tried to read his notes in the hope of memorising some of them. They made sense, but not the kind of sense he needed. Most of his attention was elsewhere. He was convinced now that the plump pale man in the train had played some sort of hypnotic trick on him. "You will see," the fellow had said, after he had imposed his will upon him in some mysterious fashion. Of course it was ridiculous to suppose that most people in Leadington were either asleep or dead. There was a trick in it somewhere. Cobthorn told himself hopefully that the hypnotic effect would probably wear off very soon. The thought of addressing a large meeting composed of the dead and the sleeping belonged to a nightmare. What a pity this fellow could not be let loose, to do his worst, among the leaders of the Opposition!

Partly because he needed another drink, and partly to see what would happen, he rang the bell again. It was answered once more by the very young waiter, and he still seemed to be asleep. Cobthorn merely gave his order the first time, but when the waiter returned with the large whisky and soda, Cobthorn had to say something.

"What's the matter with you?" he demanded irritably.

"Plees—sare—what you mean?" stammered the waiter, looking frightened. But in spite of the anxious stammer and the frightened look, he did not seem to be awake.

"You're half asleep," said Cobthorn severely.

The waiter protested almost violently, and there was more than a hint of perspiration on his smooth olive forehead. He was wide awake, he declared, and indeed very busy, serving two whole floors. And Cobthorn had to admit to himself that in one sense it was very unjust to accuse the youth in this fashion. There was nothing superficially somnolent about him; clearly he was anxious to do his duty. Nevertheless he still seemed, even in his sweat and fear, to belong to some great sleep-walking population. It was this thought that alarmed Cobthorn, after he had let the waiter go. For this was obviously what the fellow in the train had meant, that there existed a point of view, which somehow he had imposed on Cobthorn, that saw whole masses of people, who imagined they were alive and awake, as either dead or asleep.

After swallowing his whisky, Cobthorn determined to defy this outrageous standard of judgment. Seizing his notes and jumping to his feet, he compelled himself to imagine that he was already on the platform in the imposing Beaconsfield Hall, still ringing with the applause of an eager audience. "Mr. Chairman—and friends," he mouthed, and swept into his speech, the old political hand, the confident Minister of the Crown. He cracked a few jokes—and could almost hear the laughter of the crowd—and then made some preliminary points. It was going well. Then he arrived at his statement of the Government's new policy, first explaining its general trend and then coming to the part his own Ministry would play. He found it was hardly necessary for him to consult his notes. The familiar phrases came smoothly and effectively; he was eloquent as well as lucid and persuasive. "I can assure you, my friends," he thundered silently, flinging out an arm and pointing a forefinger at a mezzotint of two Regency lovers that tried to decorate the opposite wall. And then he stopped—frozen with horror. For it seemed to him then that he *had been talking in his sleep.*

Miserably he debated with himself. Should he remain in this cheerless room, trying to fight this appalling hypnotic effect, or should he risk everything and go down and eat in the dining-room, where the spell might be broken? Of course if it was not broken, then he would be worse off than before, almost imprisoned for the evening in this horrible idea. But he could do no more up here, and besides, he was hungry. So he rang down to ask for a table, and did some brisk washing and brushing.

The main dining-room of the Midland Hotel, Leadington,

is a large room, and although its style suggests an uneasy compromise between an Indian palace and a municipal swimming bath, it is very popular and is nearly always full. Palms in the middle provide shelter for waggons of doubtful *hors d'œuvres* and stewed fruit and custard. A trio of distressed gentlewomen play the melodies of Noël Coward and other master-works of our age. Cobthorn, his brow clouded with political profundities and top secrets, marched to his table, which was nicely equidistant between the palms and the trio. He saw that the place was well-filled, but at first ignored his fellow-diners and hastily ordered a light meal and some more whisky. For a few minutes he felt much better. It looked as if the sensible world had returned. He knew that he had been recognised, and was careful to look his public self. The Brown Windsor came and went. So far, so good. Then he took a hefty swig of whisky and decided that he could risk giving the other people there his full attention.

The result was disaster. Of the hundred or so in that room, apparently only three were alive and awake: a small boy dining with his parents, both sound asleep; an elderly man playing host to three others, all dead; and the woman who played the 'cello in the trio. Of the rest, waiters and all, about a quarter were dead and could have been buried, and the remaining three-quarters were all eating and drinking and chattering and staring in their sleep. Cobthorn saw all this quite clearly. He noticed too that the whole room, together with everybody in it, seemed much further away from him than it would have done at any other time. Part of him did not seem to be *in* the room but poised somewhere above it, looking down into it with an appalling clarity of vision. A nightmare experience.

If in despair he took his attention away, concentrating on himself at the table, sombre reflections darkened his mind like storm clouds. His whole career seemed a monument of futility. He and his friends were put into power by voters sleep-walking to the polls. They themselves acted and talked in their long sleep, going round and round, in office or out of it, with their eyes closed. The nations slumberingly demanded peace and moved inevitably in a trance towards war. Every argument for or against every policy appeared to be nothing but the muttering of somnambulists. What was he but the Minister of a department lost in a dream? Editors who had not been awake since childhood ordered leading articles to praise or blame him. Cabinets met like the victims of some stage hypnotist. There were senior Ministers, he realised now, who had been dead for years. To pretend that anything vital was being accomplished was manifestly absurd. There had been times before, when he had felt tired and depressed, when he had not been able to escape the feeling that nothing real could be done; now he saw clearly that they were all deluding themselves, that all the fuss and worry and shouting were quite useless, that genuine freedom of action was a dream, that they were all pawns imagining in their conceit that they were chess players, that the unexpected and terrible ends that were achieved came from moves made in some invisible world. And—a bitter reflection, turning the knife in the wounded ego—the only people who were alive and awake, free of this curse that had overtaken the world, were a few odds and ends of nonentities, a seedy magician mistaken for a crank, an elderly waiter, a boy, a fourth-rate 'cellist.

"Enjoyed your dinner, Sir George?" asked the head-waiter, out of his walking grave.

"No." And the great man stalked out, his gaze fixed on the glass doors ahead, which were being opened and closed by a page boy, already sinking into his lifelong sleep.

Old Douglas Jerdan and Morrow were waiting for him in the entrance hall. He found himself hating the sight of them. Morrow still seemed asleep, and Jerdan if anything seemed deader than before. What a precious pair! But—he had to ask himself in all fairness—was he much better? Just when he had appeared to be rehearsing his speech in his best style, hadn't he suddenly discovered he was really doing it in his sleep? But later, when he was pretending to be talking or listening to the dead man and the sleeper by his side in the Rolls, on their way to the hall, he reminded himself that most of tonight's audience would be asleep too, so that there was no reason why he should make a fool of himself. If he were faced with rows and rows of people all fully alive and awake, who looked at him as that fellow in the train had done, that really would be something to worry about; but the odds, he reflected cynically, were heavily against there being such an audience at any political meeting. So all he had to do, he decided as they drove up to the back door of the hall, was to keep calm, try to forget about this dead and sleeping business, and at least give a show of making an important political speech.

"We've a strong platform, Sir George," said Morrow out of his Party agent's dream. "Both our local members, and all the chairmen and secretaries of the district branches. They'll all be waiting for you upstairs here, and you've time to have a word with some of them."

Cobthorn grunted some sort of acknowledgment. Most of these people bored him at any time, and tonight, if he was still trapped in this horrible vision of humanity, they would be nothing more than an assortment of the sleeping and the dead, with perhaps a higher proportion of the dead than he had yet discovered. Climbing the steps up to the long room behind the platform, he braced himself to meet them. He could hear the organ thundering and wheezing away, joining the audience in declaring that there would always be an England. And what an idiotic whining song that was—a world away from the old and genuinely confident patriotic songs!

There they were, just as he had expected, the dead old men and the sleep-walkers and sleep-talkers. But there was the unexpected twist, just to make things more difficult. This time it was a woman, a plain middle-aged woman, the wife of one of the local members, Frank Marley. Jovial Frank, one of the wags of the Party and the House, turned out to be one of the deepest sleepers he had met that day; but Mrs. Marley, whom he had never seen before, was a very different matter.

"Never attends a big meeting," said Frank, after the introduction, "but she suddenly decided—at the last minute—she'd come tonight. So you ought to feel honoured, George."

"Oh—I do, I am," Cobthorn heard himself crying. He looked at her. "What made you change your mind?"

She held his glance, fixed it. "I was curious to know what you were going to say, Sir George," she told him, smiling.

It was the same smile, the same look. In one flash of discernment, he realised without a shadow of doubt that *she knew*. Not only that but she instantly discovered that he realised she knew.

"Don't you find Leadington a dead-alive sleepy sort of place?" she enquired, still holding his glance.

"No, I don't," he cried violently, trying to escape her look, at once searching and teasing. "Isn't it time we went in?"

It was. The dead and the sleepers lined up. Cobthorn was relieved to be free of the appalling Mrs. Marley, who might have been sent to the meeting by that smiling sorcerer in the train; but try as he might to forget it, he could still feel, like a cold draught on the back of his head, the influence of her presence. Going on to the platform, he made the greatest effort yet, and for the first minute or two this was a big meeting like any other. The hall was well-filled with people who seemed anxious to hear him, for the applause was no mere polite token but the real heartening thing. The atmosphere was right. The audience was a proper audience; the platform was indeed so much genuine strong local support; the chairman was that fine old Party stalwart, Douglas Jerdan, looking like an elder statesman; and he was himself again, the principal speaker, the coming man who had arrived, Her Majesty's Minister and Privy Councillor, Sir George Cobthorn, with a sheaf of notes on his knee that would soon set the men at the Press tables below enthusiastically scribbling. Yes, for a minute or two, while the clapping continued and old Jerdan rose to silence it, all was well.

Then, in that fearful twinkling of an eye against which we

have all been warned, the sensible world vanished and in its place was the nightmare vision, now stronger, more sinister, than ever. Old Jerdan, there could be no doubt about it, was simply a talking corpse, making the stiff gestures of a *revenant*: his place was not the platform but the vault. All around him the sleepers slept, nodding their foolish heads in a dream, and the dead waited for the graves to open for them. Down below and high above in the balconies, faintly *hear-hearing* and remotely clapping their idiot hands, were row upon row of men and women who had not been awake since childhood, who in two senseless hours from now would move in a trance out of the hall and go blindly into cars and buses, plunge into the deeper sleep of the night and then imagine in the morning light that they were really awake. From somewhere behind him came a cough, small and dry but curiously full of meaning, and he turned—to meet the same look, the same smile—Mrs. Marley, it seemed, reminding him again that most people in Leadington, like most people elsewhere, were either asleep or dead. And it was true, it was true; and as he turned and stared into the body of the hall, he seemed to see millions and millions and millions all sleeping their lives away while the world they had no hope of controlling went spiralling down to meet unimaginable disasters. What could he say? What could he do?

"... And now ... great pleasure ... privilege ... without more ado," droned the corpse of Douglas Jerdan, "to ask ... distinguished speaker ... Her Majesty's Minister ... Sir George Cobthorn. ..."

They were clapping again, far far away out of their dream of living. He was standing. He was moving forward a pace or two. Silence at last, the silence of sleep, the silence of death. "Mr. Chairman—and friends——" Had he spoken yet or was he dreaming he had started his speech? He was never to be certain.

The hall was a buzz that soon became an uproar. The reporters at the Press tables, the men and women on the platform, the people in the front rows were jumping up and gaping and exclaiming. For there was Sir George Cobthorn, his eyes glassy in a face like paper, waving his arms like a lunatic, and screaming "Wake up! Wake up! Wake up!"

MR. STRENBERRY'S TALE

"AND THANK *you*," said the landlady, with the mechanical cheerfulness of her kind. She pushed across the counter one shilling and four coppers, which all contrived to get wet on the journey. "Yes, it's quiet enough. Sort of weather to bring them in too, though it's a bit early yet for our lot. Who's in the Private Bar?" She craned her fat little neck, peered across the other side, and then returned, looking very confidential. "Only one. But he's one of our reg'lar's. A bit too reg'lar, if you ask me, Mr. Strenberry is."

I put down my glass, and glanced out, through the open door. All I could see was a piece of wet road. The rain was falling now with that precision which suggests it will go on for ever. It was darker too. "And who is Mr. Strenberry?" I enquired, merely for want of something better to do. It did not matter to me who Mr. Strenberry was.

The landlady leaned forward a little. "He's the schoolmaster from down the road," she replied, in a delighted whisper. "Been here—oh, lemme see—it must be four years, might be five. Came from London here. Yes, that's where he came from, London. Sydenham, near the Crystal Palace, that's his home. I know because he's told me so himself, and I've a sister that's lived near there these twenty years."

I said nothing. There did not seem to be anything to say. The fact that the local schoolmaster came from Sydenham left me as uninterested as it found me. So I merely nodded, took another sip, and filled a pipe.

The landlady glanced at me with a faint reproach in her silly prominent eyes. "And he's queer is Mr. Strenberry," she added, with something like defiance. "Oh yes, he's queer enough. Clever, y'know—in a sort of way, book-learning and all that, if you follow my meanin'—but, well—he's queer."

"In what way is he queer?" It was the least I could do.

She put her hand up to her mouth. "His wife left him. That's about two years ago. Took their little boy with her too. Gone to stay with relations, it was given out, but we all knew. She left him all right. Just walked out one fine morning and the little boy with her. Nice little boy, too, he was. He lives alone now, Mr. Strenberry. And a nice mess, too, I'll be bound. Just look at his clothes. He won't be schoolmastering here much longer neither. He's been given a few warnings, that I do know. And you can't blame 'em, can you?"

I replied, with the melancholy resignation that was expected of me, that I could not blame them. Clearly, Mr. Strenberry, with his nice mess, his clothes, his general queerness, would not do.

The landlady shook her head and tightened her lips. "It's the same old trouble now. Taking too much. I don't say getting drunk—because, as far as I can see, he doesn't—but still, taking too much, too reg'lar with it. A lot o' people, temperancers and that sort," she went on, bitterly, "think we want to push it down customers' throats. All lies. I never knew anybody that kept a decent house that didn't want people to go steady with it. I've dropped a few hints to Mr. Strenberry, but he takes no notice. And what can you do? If he's quiet, behaves himself, and wants it, he's got to have it, hasn't he? We can't stop him. However, I don't want to say too much. And anyhow it isn't just what he takes that makes him queer. It's the way he goes on, and what he says—when he feels like saying anything, and that's not often."

"You mean, he talks queerly?" I said, casually. Perhaps a man of ideas, Mr. Strenberry.

"He might go a week, he might go a fortnight, and not a word—except 'Good evening' or 'Thank you', for he's always the gentleman in here, I must say—will you get out of him. Some of the lively ones try to draw him out a bit, pull his leg, as you might say—but not a word. Then, all of a sudden, he'll let himself go, talk your head off. And you never heard such stuff. I don't say I've heard much of it myself because I haven't the time to listen to it and I can't be bothered with it, but some of the other customers have told me. If you ask me, it's a bit of a shame, the way they go on, because it's getting to be a case of——" And here she tapped her forehead significantly. "Mind you, it may have been his queerness that started all his troubles, his wife leaving him and all that. There's several that knows him better than I do will tell you that. Brought it all on himself, they say. But it does seem a pity, doesn't it?"

She looked at me mournfully for about a second and a half, then became brisk and cheerful again. "He's in there now," she added, and bustled away to the other side of the bar, where two carters were demanding half-pints.

I went to the outer door and stood there a moment, watching the persistent rain. It looked as if I should not be able to make a move for at least half an hour. So I ordered another drink and asked the landlady to serve it in the Private Bar, where Mr. Strenberry was hiding his queerness. Then I followed her and took a seat near the window, only a few feet away from Mr. Strenberry.

He was sitting there behind a nearly empty glass, with an unlighted stump of cigarette drooping from a corner of his mouth. Everything about him was drooping. He was a tall, slack, straggling sort of fellow; his thin greying hair fell forward in front; his nose was long, with something pendulous about its reddened tip; his moustache drooped wearily; and even his chin fell away, as if in despair. His eyes had that boiled look common to all persevering topers.

"Miserable day," I told him.

"It is," he said. "Rotten day." He had a high-pitched but slightly husky voice, and I imagined that its characteristic tone would probably be querulous.

There was silence then, or at least nothing but the sound of the rain outside and the murmur of voices from the bar. I stared at the Highlanders and the hunting men who, from various parts of the room, invited you to try somebody's whisky and somebody else's port.

"Got a match?" said Mr. Strenberry, after fumbling in his pockets.

I handed him my matchbox and took the opportunity of moving a little nearer. It was obvious that that stump of cigarette would not last him more than half a minute, so I offered him my cigarette-case too.

"Very quiet in here," I remarked.

"For once," he replied, a kind of weak sneer lighting up his face. "Lucky for us too. There are more fools in this town than in most, and they all come in here. Lot of loud-mouthed idiots. I won't talk to 'em, won't waste my breath on 'em. They think there's something wrong with me here. They *would*." He carefully drained his glass, set it down, then pushed it away.

I hastened to finish my glass of bitter. Then I made a pretence of examining the weather. "Looks as if I shall have to keep under cover for another quarter of an hour or so," I said carefully. "I'm going to have another drink. Won't you join me?"

After a little vague humming and spluttering, he said he would, and thanked me. He asked for a double whisky and a small soda.

"And so you find the people here very stupid?" I said, after we had taken toll of our fresh supply of drink. "They often are in these small towns."

"All idiots," he muttered. "Not a man with an educated mind amongst them. But then—education! It's a farce, that's all it is, a farce. I come in here—I must go somewhere, you know—and I sit in a corner and say nothing. I know what they're beginning to think. Oh, I've seen them—nudging, you know, giving each other the wink. I don't care. One time I would have cared. Now I don't. It doesn't matter. Nothing matters, really."

I objected mildly to this pessimism.

"I know," he went on, looking at me sombrely. "You needn't tell me. I can see you're an intelligent man, so it's different.

But you can't argue with me, and I'll tell you why. You see, you don't know what I know. Oh, I don't care if they do think I'm queer. I *am* queer. And so would you be if you'd seen what I've seen. They wouldn't because they wouldn't have the sense. . . ." His voice trailed away. He shrugged his thin sloping shoulders. His face took on a certain obstinate look that you often see on the faces of weak men. Evidently he thought he had said too much.

I was curious now. "I don't see what you mean," I began. "No doubt you've had unpleasant experiences, but then most of us have at some time or other." I looked at him expectantly.

"I don't mean that," he said, raising his voice and adding a touch of scorn. "This is different. You wouldn't understand, unless I told you it all. Even then you mightn't. It's difficult. Oh, what's the use!" He finished his whisky in one quick gulp.

"Well, I wish you'd tell me."

Doubtfully, mournfully, he examined my face, then he stared about the room, pulling his straggling and drooping moustache. "Could I have another cigarette?" he asked, finally. When he had lit it, he blew out a cloud of smoke, then looked at me again.

"I've seen something nobody else has seen," said Mr. Strenberry. "I've seen the end of it all, all this," he waved a hand and gave a bitter little laugh, "building houses, factories, education, public health, churches, drinking in pubs, getting children, walking in fields, everything, every mortal blessed thing. That's what I've seen, a glimpse anyhow. Finish! Finish! The End!"

"It sounds like doomsday," I told him.

"And that's what it was," cried Mr. Strenberry, his face lighting up strangely. "Anyhow, that's what it amounted to. I can't think about anything else. And you couldn't either, if you'd been there. I've gone back to it, thought about it, thought round and round it, oh, thousands of times! Do you know Opperton Heath? You do? Well, that's where it happened, nearly three years ago. That's all, three years ago.

I'd gone up there for a walk and to have a look at the birds. I used to be very interested in birds—my God, I've dropped that now—and there are one or two rare kinds up on the Heath there. You know what it's like—lonely. I hadn't met a soul all afternoon. That's the worst of it. If there'd only been some-body else there——"

He broke off, took up his smouldering cigarette, put it down again and stared in front of him. I kept quiet, afraid that a chance word might suddenly shut him up altogether.

"It was a warm afternoon," he said, beginning again as abruptly as he had stopped, "and I was lying on the grass, smoking. I remember I was wondering whether to hurry back and get home in time for tea or to stay where I was and not bother about tea. And I wish to God I'd decided to go back, before it happened. But I didn't. There I was, warm, a bit drowsy, just looking at the Heath. Not a soul in sight. Very quiet. If I could write poetry, I'd write a poem about the Heath as I saw it then, before the thing happened. It's all I would write too. The last five minutes there." He broke off again, and I believe there were tears in his eyes. He looked a figure of maudlin self-pity, but nevertheless it may have been the lost peace and beauty of the world that conjured up those tears. I did not know then. I do not know now.

"Then I saw something," said Mr. Strenberry. "It was a sort of disturbance in the air, not fifty yards from where I was. I didn't take much notice at first, because you get that flickering on a warm day up there. But this went on. I can't describe it properly, not to make you see it. But in a minute or two, you couldn't help noticing it. Like a thin revolving column of air. A waterspout made of air, if you see what I mean? And there was something dark, something solid, in the centre of it. I thought it must have something to do with a meteor. I got up and went closer, cautiously, you know, taking no chances. It didn't seem to be affecting anything else. There was no wind or anything. Everything was as quiet as it was before. But this column of air was more definite now, though I can't exactly explain how it came to look so definite. But you knew it was there all right, like seeing one piece of glass against another piece. Only there was movement in this, and faster than the fastest piece of machinery you ever set eyes on. And that dark thing in the centre was solider every second. I went closer still. And then the movement inside the column—like a glassy sort of pillar it was, though that doesn't quite give you the idea—stopped, though there was still a flickering and whirling on the outside. I could see that dark thing plainly now. It was a man—a sort of man."

Mr. Strenberry shut his eyes, put his hands up to them, and leaned forward on his elbows. In the quiet that followed I could hear two fellows laughing in the bar outside. They were shouting something about a litter of pigs.

"He was a lightish greeny-blue in colour, this man," Mr. Strenberry continued, "and the same all over. He'd no clothes on, but I got the idea that he'd a very tough skin, leathery, y'know. It shone a bit too. He'd no hair on him at all, and didn't look as if he'd shaved it all off but as if he'd never had any. He was bigger than me, bigger than you, but no giant. I should say he was about the size and figure of one of your big heavyweight boxers—except for his head. He'd a tremendous head—and of course as bald as an egg—and a wonderful face. I can see it now. It was flattish, like some of the faces of the Egyptian statues in the British Museum, but what you noticed the minute you saw it were the eyes. They were more like a beautiful woman's eyes than a man's, very big and soft, y'know, but bigger and softer than any woman's eyes—and such a colour, a kind of dark purple. Full of intelligence too. Blazing with it, I knew that at once. In fact, I could see that this man was as far above me as I am above a Hottentot. More highly developed, y'know. I'm not saying this because of what I learned afterwards. I saw it at once. You couldn't mistake it. This greeny-blue hairless man knew a million things we'd never heard of, and you could see it in his eyes. Well, there he was, and he stared at me and I stared at him."

"Go on," I said, for Mr. Strenberry had stopped and was now busy staring at me.

"This is the part you've got to try and understand," he cried, excitedly. "You see, this queer revolving cylinder of air was between us, and if it had been glass two feet thick it couldn't have separated us any better. I couldn't get at him. I don't say I tried very hard at first; I was too surprised and frightened. But I did try to get nearer after a minute or two, but I couldn't, and I can't possibly explain to you—no, not if I tried for a week—how I was stopped. Call it a transparent wall, if you like, but that doesn't give you the idea of it. Anyhow, it doesn't matter about me. The point is, he couldn't get out, and he obviously knew more about it than I did, and he was trying desperately hard. He'd got some sort of little instrument in each hand—I could see them flash—and he kept bringing these together. He was terribly agitated. But he couldn't get out. He'd stopped the inside of this column revolving, as I said, but apparently he couldn't stop the outside, which was whirling and whirling just as fast as ever.

"I've asked myself thousands of times," Mr. Strenberry went on, more reflectively now, "what would have happened if he had got out. Would he have ruled the whole world, knowing so much more than we do? Or would these fools have shoved him into a cage, made a show of him, and finally killed him? Though I don't imagine they could have done that, not with this man. And then again, could he have existed at all once he had got out? I don't mean just microbes and things, though they might easily have killed him off, because I don't suppose his body knew anything about such a germ-ridden atmosphere as ours. No, I don't mean that. This is the point. If he'd got out, really burst into this twentieth-century world, he might have stopped existing at all, just vanished into nothing, because, after all, this twentieth century isn't just a date, it's also a condition, a state of things, and—you see—it doesn't include him. Though, of course, in a sense it does—or it did—because there he was, on the Heath that day."

"I'm afraid I don't follow all this," I said. "But go on, perhaps it will become clearer."

Mr. Strenberry leaned forward and fixed me with his little boiled eyes. "Don't you see, this man had come from the future? Fellows like H. G. Wells have always been writing about us taking a jump into the future, to have a look at our distant descendants, but of course we don't. We can't; we don't know enough. But what about them, taking a jump into the past, to have a look at us? That's far more likely, when you come to think of it. But I don't mean that is what this man was doing. He was trying to do more than that. If you ask me, they'd often taken a peep at us, and at our great-great-grand-parents, and for that matter at our great-great-grandchildren too. But he wasn't just doing that. He was trying to get out, to escape from his own time altogether."

I drew in a long breath, then blew it out again, slowly.

"Don't you think I'm merely guessing that," cried Mr. Strenberry, "because I'm not. I *know*. And I know because he told me. I don't mean to say we talked. As a matter of fact, I did try shouting at him—asking him who he was and where he'd come from, and all that—but I don't think he heard me, and if he did, he certainly didn't understand. But don't make any mistake—he saw me all right. He looked at me just as I looked at him. He made a sign or two, and might have made more if he hadn't been so busy with those instruments and so desperately agitated. He didn't shout at me, never opened his lips. But he *thought* at me. That's the only way I can describe it. Messages from him arrived in my head, and turned them-selves into my own words, and even little pictures. And it was horrible—horrible, I tell you. Everything was finished, and he was trying to escape. The only way he could do it was to try and jump back into the past, out of the way. There wasn't much of the world left, fit to live in. Just one biggish island, not belonging to any of the continents we know—they'd all gone, long ago. I don't know the date. That never came through, and if it had, I don't suppose it would have told me much. But it was a long time ahead—perhaps twenty thousand years, perhaps fifty thousand, perhaps more—I don't know. What I do know is that this man wasn't anybody very important, just a sort of minor assistant in some kind of laboratory where they specialised in time experiments, quite a low-class fellow among his own kind, though he would have seemed a demi-god to me and you. And I knew that while he was so terrified that he was frantic in his attempt to escape, at the same time he was ashamed of himself, too—felt he was a kind of dodger, you see. But even then, what was happening was so ghastly that he'd never hesitated at all. He had run to the laboratory or whatever it was, and just had time to jump back through the ages. He was in terror. He didn't show it as we might, but I tell you—his mind was *screaming*. Some place—a city, I think it was—had been entirely destroyed and everything else was going too, everything that had once been human. No words came into my mind to describe what it was that was destroying everything and terrifying him. Perhaps I hadn't any words that would fit in. All I got were some little pictures, very blurred, just like bits of a nightmare. There were great black things rolling about, just wiping everything out. Not like anything you've ever seen. You couldn't give them a shape."

Here Mr. Strenberry leaned further forward still, grasped my coat-sleeve, and lowered his voice.

"They weren't beasts or huge insects even," he whispered. "They weren't anything you could put a name to. I don't believe they belonged to this world at all. And something he thought rather suggested that too. They came from some other place, from another planet perhaps. Don't you see, it was all finished here. They were blotting it out, great rolling black things—oh, horrible! Just imagine what he felt, this man, who had just managed to escape from them, but now couldn't get out, into this world and time of ours. Because he couldn't, that was the awful thing. He tried and tried, but it couldn't be done. And he hadn't long to try either, I knew that. Because of what was happening at the other end, you see. I tell you, I stood there, looking at him, with his thoughts buzzing round my own head, and the sweat was streaming down my face. I was terrified too, in a panic. And then he was in an agony of fear, and so was I. It was all up. The inside of that column of air began revolving again, just as it had done when it first came, and then I couldn't see him distinctly. Only his eyes. Just those eyes, staring out of the swirl. And then, I saw something. I swear I did. Something black. Just a glimpse. That's all. A bit of one of those things, getting hold of him—the last man left. That's what it must have been, though how I came to see it I don't quite know, but I've worked it out this way and that way, and it seems to me——"

"A-ha, who have we here?" cried a loud, cheerful voice. "How's things, Mr. Strenberry?"

Two red-faced men had just entered the room. They grinned at my companion, then winked at one another.

"A nasty day, Mr. Strenberry," said the other fellow. "What do you say?"

Mr. Strenberry, who appeared to have crumpled up at their approach, merely muttered something in reply. Then, giving me a hasty glance, in which shame and despair and scorn were mingled, he suddenly rose and shuffled out of the room.

The two newcomers looked at one another, laughed, and then settled into their corner. The landlady appeared with their drinks. I stood up and looked out of the window. The downpour had dwindled to a few scattered drops, brightening in the sunlight.

"I seen you talking to Mr. Strenberry," the landlady said to me. "Least, I seen him talking to you. Got him going, too, you did. He's a queer one, isn't he? Didn't I tell you he was a queer one? Telling you one of his tales, I'll be bound. Take no notice of him, mister. You can't believe a single word he says. We found that out long since. That's why he doesn't want to talk to us any more. He knows we've got a pinch of salt ready, Mr. Strenberry does."

NIGHT SEQUENCE

I

. . . AND THEN—this was the pay-off—he reversed so hard that they went into a ditch. It was a shallow ditch and they were in no danger. But the car would not budge, and the rear end of it, with all their luggage at the back, was well under water. With some difficulty, for the car was at a sharp angle and outside it was nothing but rain and darkness, they climbed out and scrambled on to the road.

"And now what?" Betty was shrill, not having recovered yet from her fright.

"Don't be a bloody fool. Why ask me?" Luke was angrier than ever. "You know all about it, don't you?"

They glared at one another through the dark and the curtain of rain between them. Idiotic, of course, but there you are. "If you hadn't got into such a foul temper when I told you that was the wrong turn," she cried, not far from tears, "you wouldn't have backed into that ditch."

"No doubt. But who wanted to come this way? What was the point? Just tell me that." He had been wet for some time, because the old canvas hood was far from being waterproof; but now the rain was running icily down his back. "No use blaming me now. Got a cigarette?"

"No, of course I haven't got a cigarette. Didn't I ask you to stop at that pub for some cigarettes—and you wouldn't?"

"Oh—for God's sake!" He stamped about in a meaningless fashion, only to realise that his shoes were full of water. He could feel it oozing between his toes. "We've had nothing to eat, nothing to drink. We're miles from anywhere. And now we can't even raise a cigarette between us."

"And whose fault is that?" she demanded.

"What the hell does it matter whose fault it is? Don't go on and on like an idiot." He could hear his voice reaching a high wobbling note, as it often did, to his disgust, when he was agitated. Why couldn't he be really tough and stay in the bass register? Why had he to be here with Betty? Why did she want to come this way? Why had he to miss the turn, reverse so savagely, land them in the ditch? Why—why—why? "We're only wasting time. The question is—what do we do now?"

"Well, that's what I was asking when you told me not to be a bloody fool—thank you very much." Betty really was crying now; it seemed even sillier than usual, seeing there was so much water about. She moved a little closer. "Can't you do anything about the car? Is it hopeless?"

"Of course it's hopeless."

"What about our bags?"

There was a time when it had made him feel proud and happy to be regarded by Betty as a kind of magician; now her helpless questioning only fed his disgust. "They're in the middle of that ditch and as far as I'm concerned that's where they're staying. If you want to try undoing those straps under water go on—try it. But I warn you that everything will be soaked. So forget 'em."

"Okay." She was the continuity girl now, not the appealing wife. "If we've had it, we've had it. Come on."

"Come on where?" he shouted angrily. The downpour was worse than ever, more like a cloudburst than ordinary autumn rain.

Betty stopped being the quiet capable continuity girl. "How do I know and what does it matter where? But we can't stand here all night, getting wetter and wetter, just screaming at each other like lunatics. We can find some sort of shelter, can't we?"

Luke admitted that they could try. It did not matter which way they went, for, as he had already announced, they were miles from anywhere. He was not sure what county they were in. Northampton, Bucks, Bedford? At the crossroads near-by, where she said he had taken the wrong turn, she moved to the right and he followed without protest. They went squelching along, through rain darkly drumming away; trudging and muttering like a pair of outcasts. Sometimes their shoulders bumped, but they left it at that, without any arm-taking or hand-holding, though they were young and had been married only three years and were not at the moment having affairs with anybody else. They might have been any two employees of the New Era Actuality Film Company, which did indeed still employ them, Luke as a director, Betty on scripts and continuity, after it had first brought them together. Stumbling on, cold now as well as wet, with his head well down, Luke thought of the job from which they were returning, the usual Documentary Short, this time on a big new cement works near Nottingham. A few nice shots, mostly long shots of the exteriors, but basically a corny job. He knew it, the unit boys knew it, and very soon the cement people and the public, if any, would know it.

"I see a light," Betty announced.

He came out of his sour reverie. "Where?" But then he saw it too. Well off the road, and rather dim. "Doesn't look promising."

"Neither does this filthy dark road," she snapped. "And I've had enough of it. At least they can tell us where we are—and let us use the 'phone if they have one."

"We might find something better round the corner." But he said this without conviction, just to raise an objection.

"Oh—don't be stupid. I'm half-drowned. There's some sort of drive there, I think."

While they were hesitating, the night turned into a black cascade, soaking them in a cold fury. Without another word, they turned in the drive at an irregular trot and splashed their way, head down and half blinded, towards the light. Luke arrived first between the two pillars, snapped on his lighter in the shelter there, and was thumping away at the massive old knocker when Betty joined him. They stood there shivering, still silent.

There was nothing remarkable, as they agreed afterwards, about the woman who opened the door: she was dumpy and elderly, dressed in black. They began explaining themselves and their plight and were still at it when they found themselves indoors and the woman, who had not spoken, was turning a key in the door, locking out the night and not them. She held a lamp up towards their faces, gave them another long look, muttered something they could not catch, and then, putting down the lamp, hurriedly left the hall, closing the door behind her. It was a square hall, not very large, sparsely furnished, with no suggestion of comfort and good cheer about it. Indeed, it was rather like an entrance to a museum.

"I hope she understood what we said," Betty muttered, wriggling a little in her discomfort. "And has gone to ask somebody what to do about us. My God—I feel like a drowned rat."

"You look like one," said Luke, without a smile.

"And what do you imagine you look like?" She was furious with him, turned away, and tried to do something with her hair, which might have been wet, dark string. The dripping old raincoat, streaked purple sweater and tweed skirt, muddy stockings, completed the picture. Luke stared at her with distaste.

"As a matter of fact you've been looking tatty all the week," he told her. "I wanted to mention it before, but hadn't time."

"You'd plenty of time to put down double gins with Bert and Mack. And you ought to see yourself. You haven't even bothered shaving today, though you've had oceans of time. Oh—I know the idea. Trying to look like the overworked director—the Hollywood touch."

"Oh—for Chrissake——"

"That's right," she said, still not looking at him. "Let's have the dialogue now. And start shouting. That's all we need to be turned out." She shook herself. "And I never felt so wet, cold and damned miserable in my life."

"Go on, then, cry. Perhaps they'll let you stay and only turn me out." This was worse than usual; but he hated himself for suddenly hating her, then found himself hating her more for making him hate himself.

She faced him, looking so bedraggled that she was almost grotesque, but very young. "I'm not going to cry. If I once started, I think I'd never stop. And it's not just this—now. It's everything. The way you went on up there with the unit. Even the work you did—lousy——"

"Oh—it was lousy, was it?"

"Yes, it was—lousy, lousy, lousy—and you know it. Then the way you'll behave when we get back. As if it wasn't bad enough, trying to exist in that crummy little flat you had to take over from Sonia and Peter——"

"*Your* friends——"

"They aren't anybody's friends. We haven't got any friends," she continued wildly. "We haven't got anything. You're thirty-two and I'm twenty-seven—and already we've had it. Why—why? Is it you? Is it me? Is it everything? I thought it was going to be all different—and it was at first——"

He nearly told her that a girl ought to pipe down when she's looking like something the cat brought in. "You can't say I didn't warn you. Right from the start. I told you I couldn't see myself marrying anybody. Though I thought it couldn't be much worse for you than living with old Charlie Tilford, which is what you were doing, more or less, at the time. That can't have been very glamorous and gay. He was old enough to have been your father—and then some."

"That matters less than you think," she retorted. "And Charlie was always kind."

"He was always plastered——"

"All right, he was plastered. And he was old." She pushed back her wet fringe, to glare at him. "But he was kind—he was sweet. We weren't always shouting at each other—like this."

"I'm not shouting," he told her. "You're doing the shouting. And if you want to go back to old Charlie, you know what to

do. That is, if you can persuade our little Mavis to move out."
He produced a laugh of sorts but did not enjoy it.

Her mouth seemed to fall open and her eyes widened,
as if to reveal some sudden desolation. Then she shook her
head slowly, still wearing this tragic mask. It was not an act,
and Luke found it very disturbing, as if Betty was turning
into somebody else. What happened next was even more
disturbing, for she began to swear at him, using the worst
language she could ever have overheard in the studio, and
she did it without heat and violence, almost like an obscene
talking doll.

"You're talking like a foul-mouthed little slut," he
announced when she had finished.

"Perhaps that's what I am." Her tone was more normal
now.

"I wouldn't be surprised."

"If I am, then it's your fault," she said. "You've turned me
into one, Luke."

"If it had been anything good, you'd have claimed the
credit yourself. But because it isn't," he continued, with a
heavy sneer, "then it's my fault. I've noticed that before about
women." Which was untrue but sounded well, he thought.

He did not deceive her. She was in fact hard to bamboozle
in this sort of mood. "You've never noticed anything about
women except the shape of their legs. So don't pretend." She
wriggled impatiently. "God—these clothes! I'll have pneu-
monia in a minute. If you'd any sense you'd know that if you
had turned me into anything we could both be proud of, I'd
have given you all the credit, adored you for it. That's what a
girl wants to do. Like Sonia with Peter."

"They're a bright example." He made it another heavy
sneer, though actually he knew what she meant.

"All right, you don't like them. And I don't much. But
they've made something together."

"What? I've never seen it."

"No, because you don't bother noticing people properly,

don't know what's happening to them, just don't take them in. That's probably what's wrong with your work now—why it's so routine and corny——"

"Who says it's routine and corny?" he shouted, furious at having his suspicions confirmed.

"I do. And I'm not the only one," she continued, with an infuriating gleam of triumph. "Ask some of your drinking chums, if you can get them to tell you the truth."

It was then that the dumpy woman in black returned, to beckon and mutter. She handed Luke a glass with liquor in it, and indicated that he should wait there, after which she took Betty through the doorway on the left. Evidently they were not to be turned out into the night, which was still drumming and roaring away. Luke tried the liquor and discovered that it was excellent old brandy. After a couple of sips there was a tiny patch of high summer inside him. He had a taste for fine objects and examined the glass itself with approval. It had that tulip shape which the French prefer for brandy, and clearly was old and of unusual quality, like the liquor it held.

By the time he had swallowed the last drop of the spirit, which seemed to release into his empty stomach a sunshine he had lost for years, he felt rather tight. Too uncomfortable in his wet clothes to sit down, he prowled round the hall, like a man left alone in a museum; but the light from the solitary small lamp was very dim. He still felt anger against Betty. If she were not with him, to show her resentment and to provoke his, it might not be bad here, a little adventure, a break in the dreary familiar pattern. But not with her under the same roof. She would keep the pattern unbroken all right. If he had not felt so wet, cold and empty, he might have hurried out into the night again, braving the rain, the darkness, the miles from anywhere, to enjoy some experience he could call his own. Slowly and resentfully he turned over these thoughts, like an idle and gloomy farm worker with a pitchfork.

The old woman came back, to lead him out as she had done Betty. But this time they used another door, which opened on to a passage as cold and nearly as narrow as the grave. At the end of this passage was a short flight of back stairs, for the use of servants and visiting riff-raff like himself. The room she showed him, the first they came to at the top of the stairs, was of no great size and appeared to be as sparsely furnished as the hall. It was lit by two tall candles, flickering in the draught. In the middle of the floor, clouding the dim gold of the candle-light with steam, was a hip bath. As soon as the woman had shown him soap and towels and had gone muttering out, Luke peeled off his sodden clothes and lowered himself into that steam. There were no other clothes in sight, not even a dress-ing-gown, but he did not care. Here was a chance to warm, clean and dry his protesting carcase. Like most young men he was usually a casual splashy fellow in a bath, never troubling to soap and scrub himself properly; but this time he was thor-ough, enjoying the hot water and finding the hip bath more encouraging to effort than the familiar kind of tub at home.

He began thinking about Betty again, not in anger now although his resentment was still there. He went back to their first encounters in the studio, then forward from them to their marriage. Had they been happy during those first months—or merely excited? Was there something wrong with her—or with him? Or were they both all right but simply no good in partnership? Or was it life itself that ought to take the blame? And now, with this question, his resentment shifted its ground. Perhaps the answer was that you asked for a colossal feature in Technicolor when all you could have was a documentary short in black and white with some lousy cheap sound effects. Life, real life, was strictly low budget.

"Come in," he shouted, without thinking, when he heard the knock. But if these people couldn't spare a bathroom for him, they couldn't grumble if they found him stark naked. However, it was a man who entered, a portly middle-aged fellow carrying a bundle of clothes. "I thought you might like a razor too, my dear sir," he announced, holding out an old-fashioned cut-throat. "Supper in about half-an-hour. One of us will bring you down. Horrid weather. Listen to it." He waved a hand towards the shuttered window, against which the rain was beating hard. "Now don't hurry. There's plenty of time, always plenty of time."

"Thanks very much," Luke was stammering. "Very good of you to look after us like this."

"My dear sir, the least we could do." A smile, a majestic wave of the hand, and he was gone.

Sitting upright in his bath, Luke still stared at the door, wondering if the candlelight had been playing tricks with eyes that needed hundred-volt lamps. What about the clothes that had been left for him? Hurriedly he dried the upper part of himself, then jumped out and perfunctorily towelled his feet and legs. He took the clothes over to the candles. Yes, they were the same—black silk knee-breeches, long stockings, pumps, a ruffled shirt—except that this cut-away tailed coat was dark green and the one worn by the man who had just gone had been brown. In this house you were expected to wear fancy dress, Regency costume for the men. Well, if shelter, brandy, a bath, dry clothes, and supper to follow were the least these people could do, then the least Luke Gosforth could do was to put on their fancy costume and try to keep a straight face about it. So after giving his feet another rub, he began pulling on the long black stockings. "Mikes a nice chynge, ducks," he muttered, breaking into his comic Cockney act; which he favoured when things took a strange turn and he was not sure quite what was happening.

2

Betty held a candle in front of the long mirror, examined her reflection there critically at first, to make certain everything fitted and there were no embarrassing disclosures; and then stepped back a pace to wonder at and enjoy what she saw. Her hair wasn't right, of course—it hadn't a clue, though she ought to be able to improve it a bit—but the general effect was terrific. She wasn't Betty Gosforth at all, and yet at the same time she felt she looked more herself, the self she was certain she possessed, than she had done for ages. Thank goodness she had good arms and shoulders and needn't be afraid (though it was a bit much, among strangers too) of this tremendous bosomy effect! She turned one way and then the other, smiling at herself over her very nice bare shoulder. The high-waisted long dress made her look much taller, more dignified than usual but more dashing and voluptuous too—a sort of Napoleonic princess. But something would have to be done with her wretched hair. She took the candle over to the dressing-table, where there was another one, and after rubbing her hair again and then combing it, she found in the little drawer below the mirror several short lengths of broad ribbon, with which she began to experiment, lost to everything at the moment but the desire to perfect her toilet.

When at last she went rustling down the broad shallow stairs, she felt peculiar, all fancy dress and glamour outside but bewildered and rather shaky within; and very hungry too. There was a man standing below, as if waiting for her. When she drew nearer, he smiled and extended a hand. Without thinking what she was doing, she put her hand into his, and allowed him to bring her to the foot of the stairs.

"Welcome," he said, still smiling and still keeping her hand in his. He was middle-aged, perhaps about fifty, and his thick springy hair had some grey in it. His face, matching his rather bulky figure, was heavy but was lightened by a quick, clear glance, which she felt at once had something very masculine about it. He was wearing some sort of stock, a ruffled shirt, a dark brown cut-away coat, black knee-breeches and stockings; but did not give the impression that he was in fancy dress. She was certain he had always worn clothes like these. And just as she was asking herself what went on in this house, as if guessing her bewilderment he continued: "My niece will be joining us in a moment. And so, I trust, will your—er—companion—husband—lover——"

"Husband," she told him, smiling too. "It's very good of you——"

"No, no, we're delighted to have company on such a night," he said, cutting her short. "And don't let us stand on ceremony. Call me Sir Edward—or even Ned if you prefer it. What shall I call you?"

"Betty." It was out before she could stop it. She had meant to tell him she was Mrs. Gosforth and to do a little more apologising, explain about the car and all that; but somehow she couldn't. And the next moment he was conducting her, with a hint of high ceremony, into a long panelled room where there was an uncommonly generous fire and several clusters of candles, so that it was filled with lovely warmth and light. At the far end of the room was a dining-table laid for four. Sir Edward placed her in a straight high-backed chair near the fire.

"I hope," he said, bending forward a little and looking deep into her eyes, "you will take a glass of sherry with me, Betty. You will? Excellent!" His voice was powerful, rich, like that of some famous actor; but it was oddly and rather disturbingly gentle too; quite different from the voices of Luke and his friends, which were much thinner and higher but also more aggressive. This man, she reflected as he went to the sideboard for the sherry, seemed to bend his voice and his look at you—not to throw them as Luke and his friends did—and if you were a woman, you could easily find this most disarmingly attractive. In spite of his age and queer costume, this Sir Edward was in fact a most attractive man.

"Allow me to observe," he said, looking down at her as they sipped the sherry, "that you look more than becoming in this dress."

"I adore it. Only of course my hair's all wrong."

"It's uncommonly short, Betty." He smiled at her. "Some new fashion—French, I'll be bound—that hasn't reached us before down here. But I've been admiring it. In this light, it looks like black midnight with a distant fire or two somewhere. If your eyes were dark," he continued, regarding her thoughtfully, "I might like your hair less. But you have grey eyes, I think——"

"Yes, they *are* grey." It occurred to her that nobody had bothered for ages about what colour her eyes were. It would have been much the same if she hadn't had eyes, only some electric seeing-apparatus. She smiled at this observant Sir Edward, using her eyes too.

"But a warm grey, surely, like a grey velvet in strong sunlight," he said slowly, his tone both gentler and richer than ever. He sounded rather wistful about it too, as if he had waited for years to stare into exactly this kind of eye and knew that it could be only a tantalising glimpse.

To hide her confusion, although it was not unpleasant, Betty drank some more sherry. It seemed much stronger than any sherry she had had for a long time. Now that Sir Edward was silent, though she knew he was still looking at her, this was the moment to explain about the car going into the ditch and perhaps to ask a cautious question or two about this house and its family and fancy dress. But somehow, when it came to the point, there did not seem any particular reason why she should.

"I call myself a gentleman," he said, almost with regret, "and so you may be sure I shan't abuse the laws of hospitality. But I must warn you, Betty, that I have a passion for Woman—and when she appears before me wearing dark hair and fine grey eyes—by Heaven—I begin to feel overmastered by that passion. So, take warning, my dear."

As she looked up at him, she asked herself if he was about to make a pass at her, and wondered wildly what she would do if he did. It just wasn't fair to a girl if a man with such a terrific line turned at once into a pouncing wolf. But all he did—and she could not have said if she felt relief or disappointment—was to give her a slow smile, and then saunter back to the sideboard to refill his glass. When he returned, he sat opposite to her, nursing his glass on his crossed knees. He looked anything but overmastered by a passion, yet something, Betty felt, still danced and flashed between them in the firelight.

"Talk to me," she said, after waiting a little time. "Don't just think it—say it." As if she had known him for ages; but it was his fault.

His heavy face came to life again. "You have an odd abrupt trick of speech, Betty——"

"I'm sorry——"

"No, no. It has a certain charm, though if you were older and plain I might not think so." He smiled at her over the glass he was slowly raising.

"Tell me what you were thinking, please, Sir Edward." There again, it came out before she had time to remember they had just met.

"I was thinking," he began carefully, "that in middle life men either begin to die—and there are many Englishmen who are dead but not buried—or turn more and more, and with increasing passion, in the mind if not always in the body, to Woman. I suspect—except perhaps for priests and philosophers—we have no other choice—it is Death or Woman. You are astonished, I gather."

"Yes, I am." She regarded him gravely. "I always think of young men wanting women."

"Young men want women as they want beef and pudding. And it may be this is what most women prefer."

"I don't think so," said Betty.

"But men of my age," Sir Edward continued, "who are still alive and are not merely solid ghosts, cheating the graveyard, see Woman as the manifestation of a sublime mystery. She is both goddess and priestess out of a strange religion. She is the other side of things taking on exquisite shape and colouring, to attract us, and speaking our language to communicate with us. She carries a diplomatic passport from the Moon. She is the last survivor of Atlantis and all the lost kingdoms. There is more in her that is at once alien, fascinating, delicious, than there is in all China. Young men, still warm from their mothers' milk, do not perceive all this. It is only when we men are growing old ourselves that we understand that Woman, though she may be all bloom and springtime, is older than we are."

"You can't look at me like that," said Betty, "and really believe what you're saying."

"Certainly I can. And there is something in you that knows what I say is true. Something that does not belong simply to you, Betty. For Betty as Betty may be shy, humble, wondering if her hair is out of place, anxious to please her company, perhaps fearful of what the night may bring——"

"How do you know that?" she cried, but not in protest against it.

"But Betty as Woman is all I have said she is. And when you can enjoy, as I can, the contrast between the simple humility of the individual girl and the pride, grandeur, and mystery of the ancient empire of Woman, then you are doubly fascinated. Then add," he went on, regarding her with a mock severity that was not without tenderness, "hair of midnight and old fires, eyes of smoke and silver—and imagine the havoc——"

A girl came into the room. Betty didn't know if she was glad or sorry to see her. It was comforting to meet another girl in this peculiar house, but even though she was only Sir Edward's niece, this girl tumbled Betty off her perch as Woman the grand and mysterious. Also, this girl was beautiful, there could be no doubt about that. She had red-gold hair, artfully tumbling in curls from a centre parting, and wide eyes of a warm hazel. Her dress was like Betty's, white and in the Empire style, but had a cunning little frill, of a pastel blue shade, that went round her bare shoulders and curved its ends in a knot on her bosom, thus shaped like an inverted heart. She was also at least two or three years younger than Betty, who had to admit that she looked a nice girl. But she would have seemed a much nicer girl if she had not looked quite so devastating.

"Uncle Ned," she announced, smiling at them sweetly, "supper's coming in."

"Betty," said Sir Edward, who was now standing, "allow

me to present my niece, Julia. I promised our other guest he would be brought down to supper. Julia, my dear, he's in the small room at the back. Run up there, please, and give him a knock."

Julia floated away, leaving Betty and Sir Edward standing together on the hearth. "She looks a charming girl," Betty murmured, looking up at him.

"She is indeed. Delightful." He waited a moment, regarding her smilingly. "But for once I'll confess I wish she weren't with me. Though of course I'm forgetting—there's your husband." He placed a finger delicately under her chin and gently tilted her face up an inch or two. "Are you in love with your husband, Betty?"

"I was. But I don't think I am now," she replied unsteadily.

"A pity."

"Yes, that's what I think. Still——" She stopped because she had no idea what else to say. She had a strong desire, which she resisted, to close her eyes, now so near to his, with their direct masculine challenge.

"The laws of hospitality," he said softly. "No need to be pedantic about them—humph?"

"Well——" And her eyes apparently closed of their own accord. What happened now was no business of hers at all.

She felt herself gently but masterfully enclosed in his arms. There was nothing violent and passionate about the kiss that followed, otherwise, passive and helpless though she felt, she might have resented it. Nevertheless, it seemed the most personal, the most directly communicating kiss she had had for a long while. It made her feel at once enormously herself and alive, and very precious too. She opened her eyes, and withdrew gently, her knees wobbling a little.

"Somewhere between the mere pecking of salutation and the groping of mouths on their way to darkness," Sir Edward observed, "is the kiss that a man and woman exchange when they are completely aware of one another's personalities and delight in them. It is the kiss of recognition, of acceptance, of tribute, beyond friendship but not yet hounded and blinded by passion. It is the kiss of love not yet ready to destroy itself in the night. Everything that can happen is there in it but kept within the bounds of what is individual and personal, this particular man, this particular woman. Do you agree, Betty?"

She did, and as she told him so, she found herself possessed by a queer thought that everything Sir Edward said to her was something she had wanted some man to say to her, although she could not have put the words into his mouth, and that he behaved as she had wanted some man to behave, even though what he did might seem to surprise her; so that in an unreasonable fashion it was all as if she had invented him, like a dream figure. Yet there was nothing hazy and dreamlike about him and this house: they were solidly before her, unexpected, fantastic, but not at all unreal. Indeed, it was the rest of the day, with its fuss and squalor, its journey through the rain and deepening darkness to nowhere, its meaningless squabbling, that now seemed unreal.

"Yes, Sir Edward," she was saying, "I've always felt that..."

3

The clothes were not a bad fit, and Luke rather fancied himself in the dark green coat. All that was wrong now was the stock or cravat or whatever it was called, which had defeated him for the last ten minutes. He was still holding it, sadly crumpled, when somebody knocked and he went to open the door. The girl looked so beautiful, it hurt.

"I'm Julia," she said, "and my uncle sent me to bring you down to supper. You must be very hungry, aren't you?"

He found some breath. "Yes, I am—rather," he stammered. "Er—my name's Luke Gosforth. Do you know how to tie one of these things? I was just giving it up."

She smiled. "I can try. Now stand quite still, please."

He did stand still but his mind was blazing and whirling. It was as if every other girl he had ever seen was nothing but a faint copy of this one, as if in fact he had never really seen a girl before. And he was the fellow who had been telling himself that life, real life, was strictly low budget. This girl burst any budget. Life had pulled something out of a bag he didn't know was there: "I'll show you, Gosforth," it had replied. By the time she had finished tying that thing, in a fragrant kaleidoscope of red-gold curls, eyes with flecks of green and gold in them, round white arms and shoulders, he felt half drunk.

"There!" She smiled at him, as if he were an emperor. "Now we'll go down. Will you bring a candle, please?"

Halfway along the passage below, no longer as cold and narrow as the grave, he stopped her. "Just a minute, please, Julia," he began, holding the lighted candle high between them. "I'm calling you Julia because that's all the name you gave me, so I hope you don't mind. I want to say first that I'm very grateful for the wonderful way you're looking after us. Thank you very much, Julia."

She looked at him without smiling, her eyes enormous and rather dark in that wavering light. "You have no need to thank me, Luke. You wanted us, I think, and here we are."

The ghost of a thought visited him then, like a cold finger tapping his spine; but he beat it down, determined to keep everything on a sensible level. "Nice of you to put it like that, Julia. But I also wanted to say this. I might find it hard to start questioning your uncle—and don't want to embarrass anybody—so before we join the others, could you just give me a quick line on the set-up here?"

"A quick line—on the set-up?" She looked as bewildered as she sounded.

Again, some moth-wing of a thought brushed his mind, and again he took a firm grip on sense and reality. "You know what I mean," he said apologetically. "No business of mine, I agree. But it might stop me making a fool of myself later. So—tell me—why are we all wearing these clothes? What goes on here?"

"What do you want to go on here?" she said, no longer bewildered. "Is this the wrong way to live? Do you wish to show us a better way?" She waited a moment, and then, when he did not answer her: "They are waiting for us, I must remind you." She put out a hand.

When his hand closed over hers, he could have shouted for joy. Everything suddenly expanded; the world was rich and wide. "Okay, don't explain anything, Julia. I don't want to know. I'll tell you this, though. I couldn't show you a better way. I couldn't show anybody anything, though I'm supposed to. I've been living like a rat in a cage." He felt a little tug. "Yes, let's go. Sorry for the hold-up."

But he halted her again just as they reached the last door. "Look, Julia," he whispered, "don't think I'm out of my mind—though perhaps I am and it might be the sort of mind to be out of. But I must talk to you alone some time tonight. I couldn't leave here without talking to you. If I did, tomorrow would be even worse than today and yesterday."

"I knew at once you were unhappy," she said softly. "Why are you?"

"That's what I want to talk about, partly. So can we get together somewhere, just the two of us? It wouldn't be the same with anybody else there. Can we, Julia?"

She nodded. "After supper. And now we must go in."

The portly fellow in the brown coat was standing before the fire, and with him was another beautiful girl, dressed more or less like Julia, but quite different, a dark mysterious creature. There are some men who seem to claim the right to be surrounded by beautiful women, and evidently this fellow was one of them.

"Prompt to the moment," he cried jubilantly. "The food's on the table. The wine's in the decanter. Luke, isn't it? I'm Sir Edward—or Ned, if it takes your fancy and we don't quarrel. Now, Luke, give Julia an arm. Come, my dear." He said this, offering an arm, to the dark mysterious beauty; and as she turned, no longer withdrawn but as smiling and gracious as a young queen, Luke saw that it was Betty. She gave him a look that was even more disturbing than her changed appearance, for it was not an angry look, an anxious or questioning look, not any look she had ever given him before as a wife: it was serene and not unfriendly but without any feeling or even any curiosity.

So they went with some ceremony down the long room to the table at the end. Luke and Sir Edward sat facing one another; and Luke had Julia upon his right and a little closer to him than Betty was, the table having been laid in this way. No servant came in. Sir Edward served the rich soup and then carved the roast chicken. Luke ate slowly, which was unusual for him, and felt that for once he was enjoying each mouthful.

After Sir Edward had begged them formally to take wine with him and had filled their glasses, he began making a speech at them, which did not surprise Luke, who had already guessed that here was a man who loved the sound of his own voice. Betty never took her eyes off the man, and gave the impression that she was willing to sit there all night listening to him orate. But to Luke's joy there was a moment when Julia turned her peach-bloom face towards him and made a tiny grimace, as if she had guessed his thought and was showing her agreement with it. God's truth—she was the honey of the world!

"You and I, my dear Luke," Sir Edward was saying, "are fortunate men to have such ladies at our elbow. But they are here, I think, because we deserve them. Not entirely, of course, for that would be impossible, but so far as men can deserve such ladies, we deserve these. We have the eyes to observe their beauty, the minds to record, to remember and praise their charms. If they are Eros, then we are Logos. The word and the deed are with us, so we have magic too. We offer them strong arms, tender hearts, and, when the wine has gone round three or four times more, minds that shall seem enchanted kingdoms to them. For they can no more do without us than we can without them."

"No, of course not," cried Betty boldly, and held out her glass to him.

"Speak to us, friend Luke," Sir Edward continued, with one eye still on Betty. "You are still young, and a noble fellow. Poetry burns in you, I see it in your eye. Come, set these ladies delicately but surely on fire. Restore to me the green but blazing madness of my youth, before I turn complete philosopher and take this table and company into Greenland. Julia, command him."

He could not hear what she said, perhaps she said nothing but only made mocking but tender motions with her lips; but her glowing look was an invitation to a new life, as if he had fallen heir to some fabulous estate. Through his mind went pattering, like rats down a corridor, the familiar staccato phrases of disillusion and fear, the double talk of the world of double gins; but not in that fashion did he speak, when he found himself standing, looking down upon them, glass in hand. The words seemed to arrive, and be roundly spoken, of their own accord.

"Ladies—Sir Edward," he heard himself saying, "all my life I have wished to be here as I am tonight. It is not true that I am a noble fellow. I am a miserable fellow. But now I am not such a miserable fellow as I have long imagined myself to be. That is because I am here, speaking to you like this." He shot a glance at Julia and what he saw in her face turned his heart over. "I did not know this was what I wanted. I only knew, though I pretended not to know and hated my pretence, that days, months, years, were hurrying past while my life was merely being endured and not lived. I drew an evil magician's circle and existed within it, watching colour drain out of the rose and fire and gold leave the sun. I disinherited myself, planned my own starvation. I was afraid of joy, so joy never came. I believed the past to be a graveyard, the future a menace. That left me with a present time that was never anything but a tasteless wafer. My life lacked spacious dimensions; there was no room in it for style, ceremony, admiration, deep feeling, and the enchantment of long vistas. There was an artist in me and I put a rope round his neck. There was a friend, and I sneered him into banishment. There was a lover, but I could not feed him with wonder and faith. I could neither love God nor defy Him. I was too corrupt for Heaven and not lively enough for Hell. I have lived, a dusty midget, on the endless desert of cement. I would have been already half an insect, lost as a man, if some unquenched spark of soul had not for ever kept alive the resentment that burned in me. No, Sir Edward, my friend—no poetry burned in me, only resentment, though that may have been the defiance of the poet dying within me. I—and all my kind—we are the resenters; and there is a terrible despair in our resentment, for while we know we have been disinherited and cheated, we also know we have contrived to disinherit and cheat ourselves. But for once, here, tonight, I am where I might always have been. I was ready to resent you, Sir Edward—to question your generosity, to mock at your offer of friendship, to make your food seem unpalatable, your wine taste sour—but now I say you are indeed the noble fellow you said I was. That lady—so richly dark and delicately glowing— is my wife, and I know now that I have never really seen her before as she is—or as she might be; and she does well to turn away from me, to look at and listen to a better man, whose eyes and tongue do not rob her of her true inheritance. As for Julia—why should I hide what I feel? All my life I have loved her. Without seeing her, without being certain she existed, I have loved her. She is the very face of beauty—and all that is gentle and good besides—and now that I have seen her and she has spoken to me, she possesses my heart for ever."

He sat down, drained his glass, then met the dazzling look that Julia was giving him. Her hand came across the table and he raised it to his lips. Then it stayed within his grasp, small and still yet as marvellously filled with life as a bird. Were the candles dimming and turning flame into smoke, or was it the sunburst of happiness inside him that made the table seem darker? Soon he was asking himself other questions. Had he really made that elaborate speech, so far removed from his customary talk, or had he merely sat there imagining himself making such a speech? Did he kiss Julia's hand and then hold it? Once he had had a dream within a dream. Was this one of them?

Certainly, candle after candle guttered and smouldered and darkness crept along the table. It was hard to see Betty now—she seemed much further away too—and it was she who was talking to them. If you could call it talking, for the words, clear and high, seemed to come floating out of her. "I am a woman," he caught, then kept his attention steady, not to miss the rest, "and now at last, when I had begun to feel our life was all a cheat, I have met a Man, and for an hour I have begun to live as a woman should live. And as she expects to live. I do not know how it is with men—and perhaps there is less difference between us than we think—but we women grow up with expectations that owe nothing to our mothers, nurses, governesses, who tell us too little of these things. Then Nature starts us flowering, but we may wither still in bud unless the society of man ripens us. The hidden pattern of our unfolding is known to us somehow, so that we see it fragmentarily in dreams, are tantalised by it, and then driven to a terrible despair, in which we care nothing if we make life hateful to all around us. We feel we possess in secret essence, waiting to be released into the air, everything that could delight a man, whatever his mood, while it delights us too. But unless we ripen, we are nothing. We are flower and fruit that must have gardeners. Because we are so much closer to Nature than man is, we know that Nature is not enough. Man must complete us, not only in his capacity as the lover but also as the creator of a society, a style of life, in which we can grow. And now I have found that Man. To leave him would be unimaginable. Not to share a roof with him even for half a day would be a little death. Dear Ned, now I can never let you go."

All the wicks in the central candelabra seemed to be smoking, and beyond them Sir Edward's face was nothing but a blur of crimson: it might have been a great mask carried in some distant torchlight procession. What was the man saying? Luke tried to concentrate his attention. "For my part, my dear," he heard, "I believe what are most necessary are style, energy and good humour. Energy without style brings barbarism. Style without energy results in corruption and death. But even style with energy, energy with style, must have good humour too, otherwise we might be Asiatic conquerors or Caesar Borgia. I do not ask for saintliness, for I am thinking of this world, which is all I know, and not the next, which may not be there and even if it is can wait for us. I ask for a cheerful temper, for unwearied tolerance and kindness, without which we could erect a hell on earth in six months. Sheer good-nature is sadly under-valued. But there must be energy behind it or it becomes torpid. And good humour and energy must express themselves in a fine style of life."

"With light, if you'll allow me to say so," Luke called down the table, "more than we have here at this moment."

"To say nothing of coffee and brandy," cried Sir Edward. And Luke could just see him rising hastily. "We must serve ourselves, but I'll do it."

Betty had risen too. "I'm coming with you, Ned." There was some urgency in her tone.

"Why not, my dear Betty, why not?" He was jovial as he reached for a candlestick. "We'll go hand-in-hand."

"But they'll come back here," Luke said to Julia as soon as they were alone. "And remember your promise. After supper, you said."

She stood up, so white, so golden, that it appeared as if she needed no light to be seen, as if light came from her. "I have not forgotten. Dear Luke! Come, you must sit by the fire while you are waiting." She led him down the room. "I shall go for coffee and brandy too—if you would like some brandy—yes? But I shall take them up to the Library, which is always warm, and there you can talk to me as long as you please. To find the Library you go up the main staircase, not the little one where your room is, turn to the right and go along the landing and then you will see a short staircase at the end, on the left, and at the top of that staircase is the Library. It has double doors, and the inner one is covered with green baize. Be there in half an hour, not sooner because there are things I must do first. Now is there anything you want here, Luke?"

"Yes," he replied ruefully, "tobacco. I smoke all the time——"

"Sit there, and you shall have tobacco," she cried, with all the bustling gaiety of a girl who is happy to be waiting upon a man. It was incredible, but there it was—she seemed as happy to be with him as he was with her. "There." And she handed him a tobacco-box and a long churchwarden clay pipe. "And don't smoke yourself into a stupor or you won't be able to talk to me. And remember—the Library in half an hour, and it's at the top of the short staircase at the end of the landing."

After she had gone he filled the churchwarden, rather clumsily for he had never been a pipe-smoker, and lit it with a brand from the dying fire. He pulled the narrow high-backed chair closer, fitted himself into it snugly, crossed his legs, and began puffing away at the fragrant Virginia tobacco. He did not look like Luke Gosforth, was not behaving like him, and now to crown all—and to the astonishment of that central recording little self which might be the essential Luke Gosforth or might be some impersonal atom of pure intelligence—he no longer thought like Luke Gosforth. His consciousness was no longer like an angry cascading stream but more like some broad placid river. The usual staccato phrases, jeering, protesting, fearful, that went crackling through his mind as he pulled at a cigarette, strode about a room or humped himself into an easy chair, were no longer tormenting him; and in their place were large serene thoughts that came floating along the river like nobly coloured barges. He discovered in himself no noticeable pieces of wisdom; yet he felt wise, and the master, not the agitated slave, of experience. It was a moment, he felt, for planning some great work that would take years and fill them with creation. He was no longer a rat in a cage, he was a man at the end of a good day. . . .

4

When Betty left Sir Edward to go up to her room, where she remembered seeing a shawl she needed now, he told her not to return down there but to look for him in the Library, at the head of the short staircase that she would find at the end of the landing. Carrying a small brass candlestick, she found her room easily enough. In all her life, she felt, she had never before known such happiness as this. There were in fact three shawls and she amused herself trying them on in different ways. After deciding on the smallest but fleeciest, she unfastened the ribbon in her hair and used her comb again. The face she saw, not too well in the light of one small candle, was the face she had always wanted to see in every mirror, the face that had been waiting in some secret store for such a time as this, a face that was at the furthest remove from the angry hag's countenance she had worn in the car. She remembered what happened in the car and the unpleasant scene she had had with Luke after they arrived here; but now all that seemed part of a dream she had had, one of those dreams both confused and wildly improbable that can yet make the dreamer feel wretched. She did not understand the events of the last hour or so, how they could come about, what sensible explanation there was of them; but then so far she had never really tried to understand them, had no desire to live in that part of the mind which could begin to make ordinary sense out of them. She was alive now, whereas only a few hours ago she had felt half dead. Why should she ask questions when she had suddenly been transformed from a hard, angry little thing into a fountain of joy? Vague memories of fairy tales returned to her, tales in which the over-curious, the obstinate enquirers, only cut themselves off from the good magic.

Now, with no more she could usefully do to herself, she

was on fire again to be with Sir Edward, in whose presence she felt herself to be lovely and gracious and almost wise. She had more than once fancied herself to be in love, not only with Luke but also before and after she had married him, with men of his sort, brittle and demanding; but always she had felt herself working up an excitement to keep the affair going, like people at a party, and had found herself hurrying away from various doubts and hesitations, pretending they did not exist; so that the whole of her was far from being completely involved, absorbed. But with Sir Edward it was as if she began from the true centre of her being, and none of the delicious excitement had to be manufactured, while at the heart of the relationship was a wonderful calm, the peace of certainty. In whatever time and place he existed, she belonged to him.

She stood still for a moment or two outside her room, carefully shielding her candle from the draught. She could hear the steady drumming of the rain and nothing else, not a sound. The house seemed immense, cavernous. She wondered whether Sir Edward had already gone up to the Library; she had never heard him pass her room; but then he might have used another staircase. This house no longer seemed the compact Queen Anne type of small mansion she had imagined it to be when she first arrived. Most houses, she reflected uneasily, appear much larger at a first glance than they seem to be on further acquaintance, whereas this house, in a disturbing fashion, began to grow, and the longer you were in it the bigger it seemed. This staircase, descending into darkness, was not the staircase the old woman had first shown her, though it led to and from the same room. Should she go and find the Library or look for Sir Edward below? Irresolutely she drifted down and halted at the foot of the stairs, hoping to hear a sound that would tell her he was still somewhere on the ground floor. Hearing nothing, then spurred by something like panic, she hurried upstairs, going as fast as her trailing skirts and the care of her precious candle-flame would allow her to go.

There was a terrifying scuttling somewhere along the landing, and after that nothing to be heard there except her heart behaving like a trapped bird. The floor was uncarpeted and its boards worn and uneven. The air along there was cold and seemingly thick with dust. Several of the bedroom doors were open, but she hurried past without so much as a glance inside. At the end she remembered to turn left up the short staircase, which brought her to a stout door that was half open, uncovering a green baize door that was closed. She knocked at this second door, waited a moment or two, then pushed it open, discovering at once that Sir Edward was not there, nothing but cold darkness. And there was a patch of cold darkness in her mind now. She went down to the landing again and heard a horrid slithering behind one of the open doors. Her happiness a bright wreck, she felt alone and afraid. She began to run; the flame she tried to shield wavered dangerously; she had to stop to allow it to burn upright again. If this inch of flame vanished, she felt she might be lost for ever.

At the head of the main staircase, which looked large enough now for some ruined opera house, she began calling to him, telling him where she was, begging him to come and find her. But all that came back were echoes, strange echoes like so much mockery. Her final call became a scream, a scream cut off by a sob. For she knew then, with a desolate finality, like a blow delivered at the heart, that it was useless to call for Sir Edward, that he was no longer in that house, no longer in any world or time where her cries could reach him.

5

After the first ten minutes or so had gone by, Luke thought that at any moment Betty and Sir Edward might return. He was not surprised, however, when they did not come back; they were probably making long speeches at one another in some kitchen or pantry. He was not carrying a watch and there seemed to be no clock in this long room; he had to guess at the half-hour Julia asked him to wait. Finally, taking two candles for good measure, he went off to find the Library. He took two wrong turnings, along narrow passages, before arriving at the main staircase, which he had not seen before. After that it was easy enough to follow Julia's instructions, turning to the right at the head of the staircase and then going along the landing until he found the short flight of stairs. And there were the double doors she had described; he could see the green baize on the inner door.

"Julia, I'm here," he cried, all joy and excitement, with a vision of the two of them talking for hours in this Library, so remote and yet so snug and companionable with its calf-lined walls. "Here I am," he shouted idiotically as he charged in, "here I am."

The room was empty, bare, and had the damp chill of an endless winter. It had been a library once, for there were still some shelves on two of the walls and even a few shabby books heaped together in one corner. Cold ashes and a litter of half-burnt paper filled the grate. Patches of damp had not merely stained the walls and ceiling but had eaten into them. There was not a single piece of furniture in the room, only an old packing case. Nobody could have read a book here for the last thirty years. It was a room that had forgotten what human beings are like. Luke felt sick with misery.

He could hear the rain and the creaking of a shutter somewhere, and that was all. It was impossible to believe now that the room he had left, still bright with the image of Julia, was only two flights of stairs away. Terrible suspicions, for which he refused to find words, came creeping into the back of his mind. What if—once you left that long room below—you could take a wrong turning in time? Where was Julia? Where was she waiting for him with that coffee and brandy? He knew—and desperately wished he didn't know—that this was the Library she meant. He began shivering: there was ice squeezing his heart.

Then he heard steps, slow dragging steps but coming nearer. He could not move, only listen. The stairs creaked. Tremulous candlelight appeared in the doorway. His welcoming shout of "Julia!" was hope against all sense, and the hope died before the last echo faded.

"Luke," said Betty as she came forward, pale, her eyes deep-set and smudged, still dressed as she had been at the supper table but without the beauty she had worn then, not even elegant any longer, just a girl wearing the wrong clothes, "Luke, I thought it must be you." She stared about her for a moment. "Yes, I knew it would look like this. I think that's why I didn't come in before. I knew somehow." She looked at him. "Were you going to meet her here?"

"Yes," he said, looking away, towards the empty shelves. "We'd arranged to talk after supper, and she told me to come up here."

"That's what he told me." She spoke without expression, as a sleep-walker might talk. "And I came as far as the door. I think I knew then."

"Knew what?"

"That he isn't here—not now. And she isn't here either, of course." She shook her head slowly. "I'm certain now there's nobody here but us. Not even that old woman—though of course she was quite different from them."

"What do you mean, Betty?" He was rather angry.

"I mean," she said carefully, "that we might see her in the morning. But we shan't see them. Not ever. Luke, don't be cross. I couldn't bear it."

"You won't have to. I'm trying to understand, that's all. And it was a hell of a shock when I charged in here expecting to see her——" He broke off.

She nodded. "You needn't tell me. It happened to me too. And that's something, I suppose—that it happened to both of us. We ought to remember that. It's important."

"Yes, but what happened? And if we're going to talk, let's get out of this morgue. Let's go downstairs—where we had supper. That room's warm." He stopped there, stared at her, changed his tone. "Or isn't it? Perhaps that's just a cold empty dump too with nothing in it but a couple of packing cases. But look—damn it!" he cried angrily, "I'm still wearing these clothes—*their* clothes. So are you. And we had supper together, didn't we, the four of us—you don't deny that?"

"No, I don't." She sounded tearful. "But, please, Luke, don't be angry about it all. Don't let's start quarrelling again. I really couldn't bear it now."

"All right, I won't, Betty. I'm not really angry, certainly not with you. But we did have supper, all four of us—and you and he and I made speeches. Or didn't we? Am I making that up?"

"You and he did. I didn't. How could I?"

"I thought you did—about what women wanted——"

"No, I just listened to you two. And talked to him a little. But that doesn't matter now. Let's go down. We can't stay here."

As they moved to the door, carrying their candles, Luke stopped and pointed. "Look at that."

"What? I don't see anything."

He jabbed a finger at the wall. "An electric light switch. And I never noticed any before." He tried it but nothing happened. "There's no longer a fitting in here, and probably the electricity's been cut off anyhow. Let's save two of these candles. Keep close to me, I know the way down."

"Did this house seem to you to get bigger and bigger?" she asked as they went down. "It did to me—just when everything began to turn sinister and awful. I think it was when there wasn't a proper time—when it wasn't *then* and hadn't got back to *now*."

"Don't let's start on that yet." He was silent for a few moments as he led the way. "I believe you when you say they're not here. I feel they're not here now. But we're still wearing these clothes—and we had supper in that long room—that I'll swear. So let's wait for more evidence."

They entered the long room at the opposite end from the table. As soon as they were inside, Luke exclaimed: "There you are! This hasn't changed. Same furniture. The fire's not quite out yet. It's exactly as I remember it. I left those two candles burning—there they are. Now let's have a look at that supper table."

It was the same table but it was not the same meal that had been eaten there. Only two chairs had been drawn up to it, not four, and clearly only two people had used these plates and cutlery. On the table were some remaining bits of tinned meat, a dry hunk of cheese and half a loaf of bread. Near one place was a small teapot, jug of milk, cup and saucer, and at the other an empty beer bottle kept company with a glass still laced with froth.

"But I drank wine," Luke protested, "and had soup, roast chicken——"

"I had pâté and an omelette," cried Betty.

"You couldn't," Luke began; but then he checked himself. "Let's go over to the fire. No point in staring at this stuff."

"These are exactly the same chairs," said Betty when they reached the hearth. "Everything here's just the same as it was. What are you looking for?"

"A round tobacco-box and a churchwarden pipe. They were here before. I used them. But they're not here now." He poked around for a minute, while Betty sat silent. "Hello! Just what I wanted."

"What have you found?" She looked towards the sideboard.

"Five cigarettes in a packet. Right at the back here. They must have been here some time—very dry and dusty—but they'll do. Want one?"

"Yes, please. Hope it isn't stealing."

"We'll make it right with somebody in the morning."

They smoked for a while without exchanging another word, both of them staring into what was left of the fire. They had the air of being survivors after some catastrophe.

"What did you want to talk to her about?" Betty asked finally.

"Anything. Everything. It didn't matter. I hadn't planned a discussion. I just wanted to be with her."

"I did with him."

"Yes, I know you did," said Luke not unamiably. "We're both in the same boat."

"That's the one thing that makes it better," she said. "It would have been much worse if it had happened just to one of us. You're not feeling jealous about him, are you?"

"Not yet, though I think I could be," he confessed.

"You're not because you're not thinking about me—you're still thinking about her."

"Do you mind?"

"No, not yet," she said. "I'm like you. It's the same for both of us. We've lost them. And I'm certain neither of them can ever be found again. So here we are, to make the best of it."

There was so little light either from the fire or the spluttering candles that they might have been sitting in the dusk of some warm cave. The night still sounded wet and wild; it was easy to imagine a new Deluge beginning out there.

"They never seemed ghostly to me, you know," said Luke, after an interval.

"They weren't ghosts." She was decisive.

"What were they, then? People in another time? I've read and heard stories about people going back in time."

"I was thinking about that," she said eagerly.

"But then they merely saw and heard things," he continued slowly, "as spectators. They didn't join in as we did. Talking, holding hands, having supper together."

"Look at the remains of that supper there. What a swiz! Typical of us and our time too."

"No, listen, Betty," he said earnestly. "We must get this bit right. You might be able to slip along the fourth dimension or whatever it is—and don't take me up on this, I'm very hazy about it—and then perhaps see people living a hundred-and-fifty years ago. But you wouldn't be really there with them, couldn't join in as we did. Otherwise, it would mean two different times—then and now—overlapping in a third and quite different sort of time, if you see what I mean."

"No, I don't really, Luke. It's much too complicated."

"I know, that's what I'm saying. It's worse than those two women at Versailles. But what *did* happen then?"

She waited a moment, then began very carefully. "This is what I think. There were two people, Sir Edward Somebody and his niece, Julia, who once lived here, and who looked and behaved like the two we saw tonight. We arrived here very tired and on edge, wondering what was going to happen to us, and then when we relaxed and put these clothes on—well, Sir Edward and Julia happened. But—no, please, listen, Luke, this is the difficult part and if you interrupt I may lose the thread of it—but we were never *really* with them. I mean, they hadn't an independent life, as real people have. They looked themselves—we didn't make up their appearance—but what they said and did was what we wanted them to say and do, as if we were playwrights and they were characters in our play——"

"Now wait a minute, Betty," he protested. "You're not going to tell me that Julia——"

"Yes, I am," she cut in sharply. "And Sir Edward too, though I hate to say so. Didn't they always behave as we wanted them to behave? Just think, Luke. I felt some of this at the time."

"You mean you've always wanted a Sir Edward?" he asked, puzzled and displeased.

"Not consciously, no," she replied, a glint of amusement in her glance. "But he must have represented important things I did want, mostly without my knowing it. Just as Julia, who was probably rather a dull girl, a Regency version of the dumb blonde, was all marvellous and magical to you. He made me feel like that, because that's what I was wanting somebody to make me feel. Not always—that's too much to expect—but at times. And all the marvellous and magical feeling you had about Julia belonged to you, came from some part of you that was beginning to feel frustrated. Don't you see, darling," she continued in a tone she had not used with him for a long time, "that we arrived here not only wet and cold and lost but feeling utterly frustrated and miserable, just angry bits of ourselves that had been worked almost to death? And the Sir Edward and Julia we met, not the ones who really lived here, were those parts we'd neglected and forgotten. So we acted in a sort of play with them. It all started because we put these clothes on and not our own. We had to behave in a different way. But we couldn't do it with each other so we had to have those two as well, to help us out."

"That doesn't quite work," he said, "though I see what you mean. He brought me the clothes. Or I thought he did. Spoke to me too—I was still in my bath then. Didn't talk about style—that was later. Did you hear that?"

"Yes," she cried eagerly, "but all that was something, I'm sure, that I hadn't quite thought out for myself but that I'd already felt. Don't you see?"

"What I do see," he said, with a defiant air, "is that it's all very well for some Regency buck to talk about style and the grand manner in living. He could cope with it, I can't. But then I haven't got my foot on anybody's face, have to pay my own way, and no kids get up in the dark to make money for me in cotton mills and coal mines. If that's what his style depends on, he can have it. I'll still go tatting round pubs and cafeterias wearing a dirty shirt and oily pants. And you'll still be in the fish queue and the two-bob seats at the cinema. But nobody can say we're living on other people's daylight. Style my foot!"

"Yes, yes, of course we couldn't live like that," she cried, "but it isn't *style your foot*. He didn't say those things. How could he? *We* said them. You said them to me. I said them to you. That was the only way we could do it—to express what we must have been feeling deep down about ourselves and our lives. And Luke—please—don't be tough and aggressive about it. We've both had enough of that, and it isn't us, but all a dreary fake anyhow. Just be quiet and think for a minute or two, remembering what we were like when we arrived here and what you felt afterwards."

"We came in wet and snarling," he said slowly, "and then

soon it was different." As he tried to remember all that had happened—and much of it was confused, incredible—he was aware of Betty watching him intently, although her eyes were invisible and her face nothing but a pale oval in that dusk of the cave.

"If people ever look back on us—our generation, I mean—and try to give a verdict on us," he said finally, "they'll have to say we had a hell of a lot of faults but at least we were trying to be honest. No pretence at all costs—that's been our slogan. No doubt we've gone too far——"

"Much too far," she cried. "I'm sick of this honesty that leaves everything looking small, ugly and mean. And there's plenty of pretence too—neurotics pretending to be tough, tired frightened people getting rough and sexy on gin. Sheer laziness and sloppiness too—the men can't bother shaving and finding a clean shirt, the girls won't take a bath and change their underclothes. Yes, I know it's all more difficult—nobody need tell *me* that—but if we only tried to stop shuffling round and slopping about, jeering at and cheapening life—if we brought to it energy and good humour and some sense of style——" And here she broke off.

He stood in front of her and took her hands in his; her hands were cold, so he brought them together and began to warm them between his encircling palms. "You felt a shiver down your spine then, didn't you?" he said softly. "So did I. It's a good thing both of us experienced whatever happened tonight. If it had been only one of us——"

"It would have been hopeless," she told him hastily. "It's because it happened to both that there's some hope for us. But love isn't just grabbing sex when you need it and sharing a bath and a frying pan. All women know that. You have to work at it, to build something."

"The trouble is," he said, "a fellow wants to knock off, to take it easy. Yes, I know, Betty, then he expects more than he's a right to expect. You can't dress a relationship in rags and kick it around, and then ask it to satisfy a sudden demand for glamour and glory. And if we stop making these demands, we may soon find ourselves in an anthill——"

"Oh—Luke—I'm sure you said something like that," she cried. "Don't you remember?"

"I remember a little time—part of a dream or some time that doesn't really belong to us—when you were a beautiful and bewitching being and I was a noble fellow, burning with poetry and waiting to show you a mind that would seem like an enchanted kingdom to you. Yes," he continued, "I remember all that and more, and I'll try never to forget. And because I'll know that you're remembering too, you'll always seem different from any other woman——"

"Oh—yes, my darling—that's what I've been trying to say——"

"What we can do I don't know, and I'm certainly not going to work it out tonight. But from now on, at least, the names of Betty and Luke Gosforth will not be found in any heats of the rat race. And now—for I'm certain we have this place to ourselves—I must find you a bed, dear Mrs. Gosforth——"

"There's a large one in that room where I dressed," said Betty, and kissed him. On the way up, she murmured sleepily: "I still don't understand about these clothes and the old woman. And they're in this world all right."

"They are," he said, "and so, with luck, tomorrow morning ought to be able to throw some light on them."

6

It was not a morning to throw much light on anything; not raining still, but with water everywhere, and even the sunlight struggling through an atmosphere that seemed as much water as air. But it brought them a Mrs. Rogers, a beaky, bird-eyed woman, one of those who cover an immense interior good-nature and desire to help with an appearance of snapping fury. She had come up from the village of her own accord; she finished drying their clothes, gave them hot water, and even contrived a rough-and-ready breakfast for them; but she never stopped giving a performance as a woman who had been press-ganged into a hideous service.

"She's a blessing and all that," said Luke, over his boiled egg, "but we'll never find out anything from her."

"Yes, we shall," Betty declared, out of her experience of the vast ruinous underworld of London chars. "Just leave it to me, darling."

"I'd have to do that anyhow. In five minutes I'm off to buy some cigarettes and to find somebody who'll pull the car out of that ditch. And give this Mrs. Rogers a pound—here you are, while I remember—but suggest she might split it with last night's old woman, if she can be found. By the way, did you ever understand anything that old woman said?"

"Not much," Betty replied. "But I'll get it all out of this Mrs. Rogers, you'll see."

An hour later, they met in the small square hall, and as he lit the cigarette she had immediately demanded, Luke said: "I've got the bags out of the car and arranged for it to be lifted and gone over. I sent a wire to the studio. And there's a taxi coming in ten minutes to take us to the station. What's your news, woman?"

"Straight from the Rogers Service, darling," she replied. "The old woman we saw last night—Mrs. Grashki, or something like that—is a Czech. She looks after this house but lives with a daughter next door to Mrs. Rogers. Last night she was working late, luckily for us—and was actually sorting out a mass of old things. This house has belonged for centuries to a family called Periton—all baronets. The present Bart—Sir Leslie—is in the diplomatic service, so he's always abroad. Well, Mrs. Grashki, who's obviously a character, thought we looked terrible last night and thought how much nicer we'd look in some of the old things she'd been sorting out. So she put some out for us. Then after filling our baths—both the boiler and the electric light plant aren't functioning—and scraping together a bit of supper for us, probably having a peep and a giggle at us, she suddenly thought she'd gone too far, took fright, and ran home. She was thoroughly soaked of course, found herself laid up with rheumatism, and sent an S.O.S. to Mrs. Rogers, who nobly responded. I'm just saying," said Betty as Mrs. Rogers marched in, "you nobly responded to Mrs. Grashki's call for help."

"I did what I could," cried Mrs. Rogers angrily, "but if you ask me, that Mrs. Grashki's not all there—playing tricks like that at her age—and not the first neither. Thinks she's still abroad, that's her trouble. But Sir Leslie took a fancy to her, being abroad a lot too. That one there's Sir Leslie's grandfather—Sir Eustace," she pointed to one of the portraits. "And I could tell you some tales of him too."

"Darling—look!" cried Betty rather shakily. She had gone to take a closer view of Sir Eustace. He went across to stand by her side, and then he felt her fingers digging into his arm until they hurt. "There—don't you see?" And in a moment he did. The portrait of Sir Edward Periton was excellent, although the sitter's brown coat did not come out too well. The portrait of Miss Julia Periton was smaller and less successful, but the tumbling red-gold curls were admirably suggested, and her white Empire dress, with its pastel blue frill that went round the bare shoulders, was not badly done at all.

"Yes," said Mrs. Rogers with some complacency, as she joined them, "there's some more—and I could tell you some tales of these Peritons."

"So could I," said Luke.

9 781948 405119